"*W*HAT busy little bee has been running to you with stories of last night's party?" Daphne asked Lord St. Felix.

"My sister was there. She said you were the center of attention, and behaving perfectly outrageously."

"What would you expect of a parvenue whose family can only be traced for two hundred years?"

"A modicum of behavior, when it is her aim to pass herself off in Society."

"Are you setting out to reform me, Your Grace?"

"I am not so quixotic. I am merely warning you."

"So now I am a knave and a rogue, am I?"

"You always were, but when you clash horns with the Prince Regent, you take on a good deal more than you can handle."

His whole aim was to best her, but he would dislike to see her disgraced and humiliated.

"Are you offering me the benefit of your advice in payment for our silence regarding your father?"

He did not answer. But he looked at her in a strange new way.

Talk of the Town

JOAN SMITH

FAWCETT CREST • NEW YORK

TALK OF THE TOWN

Published by Fawcett Crest Books, a unit of CBS Publications, the Consumer Publishing Division of CBS Inc.

ISBN: 0-449-24137-8

Printed in the United States of America

10 9 8 7 6 5 4 3 2 1

One

MOST families have a black sheep to boast or complain of—a relative who has gone astray from the path of respectability—but Daphne Ingleside felt unique in that their family's erring member was a female, a black ewe. Aunt Effie, Mama's only sister, had been a creature of much interest to Daphne for as long as she could remember. It seemed impossible to credit that plain, and really very ordinary Mama should have a sister who had set the whole of England and half of Europe ablaze with her affairs, but so it was. Not content with marrying a very eligible earl during her first Season, she had served him false in the second year of their marriage and been caught *in flagrante delicto* with an even more prestigious gentleman, the Marquis of Ansquith, who was also married. Lord Standington, Effie's husband, who

5

served as the villain in the Ingleside version of the story, had behaved in a most ungentlemanly manner and cast off his wife in a divorce trial that had rocked the country some thirty years ago, despite the fact that he kept a whole aviary of ladybirds himself.

The Black Ewe had been severely punished for what was then her one straying from the path of wifely devotion: divorced, publicly disgraced, made a mockery of by all her former great friends. Not one of them spoke to her and, with her head bent low, she had set off for the Continent, to live out her life in sackcloth and ashes. But as luck would have it, Effie, who was allowed to retain the nominal dignity of Countess of Standington, no sooner set foot in France than she caught the eye and soon the heart of a certain Mr. Eglinton, a nabob who had made a colossal fortune with the East India Company. She felt it unbecoming to remarry, and in her deepest heart of hearts she still had a soft corner for her ex-husband. Indeed Effie's whole heart was a cotton ball of softness, according to Mama. Always the kindest, most generous of sisters. As she wended her penitential way from France to Italy, she picked up such a throng of admirers that it soon became necessary for her to remarry for her own safety, and she did so in Florence.

"The men wouldn't let her alone," Mama would sigh with satisfaction and perhaps a tinge of jealousy. Mama was not cursed with inspiring this sort of passion herself. Her husband, Sir James Ingleside, and no one else had found her irresistible. And to tell the truth, Papa was an old stick. One loved him, of course, but his whole discourse with his family was a series of complaints and commands. He was a very caring father, not only to his children but also to his wife. While poor Mama was told to eat up her peas and to stick a scarf into the neck of that low-cut gown, Effie enjoyed a foreign life of ease and recklessness. But in Greece, Mr. Eglinton had contracted a putrid fever while digging up a statue in a swamp, and with her head again bent low, Effie brought him home to England to be treated by the best doctors in the world, who soon had him in his grave. There was Effie once more, Mrs. Gerald Eglinton now, her title relinquished, cast upon a friendless sea of money. When he divorced his wife, Lord Standington retreated to his estate in Ireland a broken man, according to Mama, gnawed by his guilty conduct towards his near-innocent wife.

With surprising alacrity, Effie's great friends returned to her. Her elegant mansion on Half Moon Street was the scene of many parties, where all but the highest sticklers attended on her. She ran a salon, an idea picked up in France, of no very high intellectual calibre, but enlivened by many gracious foreigners, much good-natured joking, and the best wine the late Mr. Eglinton's money could buy. Her open-handedness was a byword. A new acquaintance need no more than mention wanting to join the Army than he was handed a commission on a silver platter. When Lady Pamela Thurston pawned her diamonds to pay her gambling debts, it was Mrs. Eglinton who got them out of hawk and said, "Pay me when you can." She put indigent friends' sons through school, lavished gifts on everyone, and thought money was only to be spent. In the space of not too

many years, she had done what she thought
should be done with nine-tenths of Mr. Eglinton's
fortune and found herself living on a small fixed
income. The champagne salons dwindled to sherry
conversazioni and the roomful of eminent guests
to three or four down-at-heels gentlemen willing to
call a plateful of macaroons and a glass of sherry
"dinner."

Mama invited her to Wiltshire, but life held yet a
few chapters for the beautiful Effie, still only in her
late twenties and with enough looks to inspire one
last passion. It was not the best of all possible
partis who succumbed to her fading charms. Mr.
Pealing was neither rich nor witty nor even very
handsome, but he was available and Effie was
lonesome, so she took him to be her third husband.
He added nothing to the patina of the legend that
had mushroomed around Effie. James had always
averred she would come to no good end and was
happy that her wayward life should stand as a
warning to his own wife and daughter. Effie's
letters now held no mention of salons or *conversazioni.* An occasional trip to Ranelagh or Vauxhall
Gardens was remarked upon, but with increasing
regularity the tone tended to be of the high prices
charged for everything. The address changed from
the mansion on Half Moon Street to Upper
Grosvenor Square, with—horror of horrors!—an
apartment number. The fabled Effie was living in
rented rooms, complaining of the cost of green
peas, not diamonds, and before too long complaining of the inefficacy of the medical profession. But
with care Mr. Pealing held on for years, and it was
not till Effie was in her fiftieth year that the long-
awaited card with its black edge informing of the

death of Mr. Pealing arrived, throwing the Ingleside household into a pelter.

"She is *all alone*," Mama pointed out to Sir James with a tear in her eye.

James's heart was made of flint. No offer was extended to Effie to share the home of her sister. "If she *asks*, we'll let her come for a visit," was the best Mama could wring out of him, and Effie never asked. She had never asked them for anything.

It was twelve months before any request came from her, and when it came, it was not to be allowed to come to them but to send her niece Daphne to her to bear her company for three months.

"Oh, Mama, I should love it of all things!" Daphne said, her dark eyes shining. Really very like Effie herself at the same age, only the eyes were grey instead of blue, and it was a shame she should not have a crack at anything but the local beaux while her youth and beauty were upon her.

"I have always wanted to meet her," Daphne said.

An accusing eye was levelled on Sir James by his spouse. "Your father does not wish her to come."

"We asked her when Eglinton died," he pointed out. "She didn't care to come to us then. Oh no, she must stay and party with her so-called friends while the money held out. It would not do at all for Daphne to go to her. An apartment in Upper Grosvenor Square! She will meet no one there."

"She is meeting no one worth a second glance here," Lady Mary retorted with a steely look. "And if Daphne is not to be allowed to go to Effie, then I shall ask my sister to come to us."

Mama occasionally got her back up at Sir James's high-handed ways; not often, but when she did, she was a perfect mule. Faced with this ultimatum, James allowed his daughter to jaunter off to London, relying on her native intelligence to keep her from mischief. Though she had the beauty of her aunt, she had, as well, a pretty fair streak of common sense from the Ingleside branch of the family. It was shown in her conversation before leaving. Unlike her goose of a mother, she did not speak of balls and routs, when she was not going to make her debut, but of wondering whether Auntie kept a carriage so that they might drive in the park. She didn't even take her ball gowns with her. This caused James a wince of regret; Daphne dearly loved a ball, and how well she danced.

"You can always have one made up should the need arise," Mama said, and slipped a little roll of bills, saved from the milk money, into her hand. She hadn't a doubt in the world that her daughter would snare a husband on this trip, and how happy she was that he might be a real gentleman and not some local squire's son.

A shared smile with her father assured him that the daughter had a clearer idea of how her visit would go. "I shall take my paints," she said. "I might do a sketch of Aunt Effie to bring back to you, and one of myself for her to keep, if she likes."

It took a week to get Daphne's wardrobe ready for her holiday, for Mama would make a half-dozen trips to the village to buy her fans and ribbons and new patent slippers, all of which she warned her were not really fashionable enough for London. She also found a pair of elbow-length blue kid gloves that she could not resist, on half price, for they had such a cityfied look to them, and it was a great pity they didn't match any of Daphne's outfits. The ancient family travelling carriage was wheeled from the stable, brushed off, washed down, and a new coat of paint given to the wheels, which were covered with dust before they'd gone two miles. Mrs. Crozier, a neighbour going to London to visit her daughter, accompanied Daphne to lend respectability on her trip, and she was off.

It was Miss Ingleside's first trip to the Metropolis, and she enjoyed every minute of it. No worries of unaired beds, outrageously high prices at inns, of highwaymen or bad food came to annoy her. She wasted her time, in Mrs. Crozier's opinion, looking out at grass, trees and fields, at passing vehicles, churches and farmhouses when she should have been figuring out whether the George at Farnborough hadn't overcharged them a shilling for their breakfast. On the third day Daphne arrived in London no more weary than if she had just gone a mile down the road, and again gazed from the coach windows at the sights. She was delighted by the busiest streets, the finest homes, the most luxurious carriages and the best-dressed people she had ever seen. This opulence was due to the fact that the coachman was also a stranger to London and not much good at reading the map Sir James had given him. He delivered his charge first to the more elite Grosvenor Square. The real estate deteriorated sharply once he found his way to Upper Grosvenor Square, but it was by no means contemptible—still perfectly respectable. Miss Ingleside felt no qualms upon entering the brick building which held her precious aunt. It looked a very common sort of a house, to be sure, to domicile Lady Standington, as Mama still frequently referred to Mrs. Pealing; but she knew her aunt to be in straitened circumstances and was prepared for it.

Within doors, Aunt Effie had been preparing for her niece for days, and all was in readiness.

Two

⸙

DAPHNE was met at the doorway by a butler
whose livery had seen better days several years
ago, but her eyes scarcely saw him; not two steps
behind was the most interesting member of her
family, the Black Ewe. She saw at a glance that the
name was an inappropriate one, for Aunt Effie
was blue, literally, from head to toe. Her hair, so
often likened to a raven's wing and Daphne's own
hair, had faded to grey and been touched up to
blue. Her eyes were blue both within and without—
the iris blue, and a blue shadow smeared on the lids
with a liberal hand. The gown was blue, and even
the feet were shod in dainty blue kid slippers.
Daphne at once perceived a recipient for the
useless blue gloves Mama had given her. The
house was also predominantly blue, and Miss
Ingleside was soon being shown into the Blue

Saloon, where blue sofas sat against blue walls on a blue carpet, with blue window hangings decorating the grey windows. The whole was dilapidated though not actually squalid.

Her surprise came out before she set a guard on her tongue. "What a *blue* room!" she said as soon as she had been made welcome.

" 'Tis but a sad relic of its former self," Effie said in a doleful tone, but she was not much given to sad repinings on the past and was soon smiling fondly on Daphne. "You are just as I knew you must be from Mary's letters," she said, admiring her niece's healthy, vivacious face, intelligent grey eyes, and reading in them the image of her own.

Her niece had to make a hard effort not to be disappointed. She knew her aunt was no longer young, but she was only fifty—five years older than Mama—and she looked sixty. There was no spark, no fire, no interestingness in her, as she was sure there must be in a lady who had led such an eventful, unconventional life. But for her blue hair and painted eyes, she might be any village matron. She was pudgy, more resigned than contented, and not even stylish. She wore an old shawl around her shoulders. Daphne felt cheated. She had come to encounter the dashing Black Ewe, and was met with a blue lap dog. She schooled herself to politeness and enquired how her aunt was enjoying London.

"Of course it's not what it once was, for *me* anyway," was the sad answer.

"Oh, dear, she's going to be a whiner," Daphne thought, and wished she were back at home. A glazed look fell on the blue eyes, and the lips lifted to reveal some barely discernible traces of a once-sweet smile. "But now that you are come, things will be better," the aunt said, rallying, and from that point on things took a little turn for the better.

"The fact of the matter is, my dear, I have been much alone since Mr. Pealing's passing. Too much alone. Solitude is very bad for you, especially if you are a shatter-brained rattle like myself, with no deep pious thoughts to sustain you. I haven't had a visitor in a month," she admitted, "nor been to see anyone. All alone but for the servants, and they, you know, only want to scold and complain."

"Oh, Ma'am, you should have come to us!" Daphne said, her sympathy touched at this news.

"And so I should have done if it weren't for that Methodist your mama married. Now pray *don't* tell me he is an Episcopalian, my dear, for I know very well what he calls himself, and what he really *is*, too. He wouldn't want a shady character like me in his house, but then I had the idea of asking Mary to send you to me, and I thought James might allow it to keep me from his door, as I make no doubt he did. But whyever you are here, I'm glad you are, for I have been dying for someone to talk to." She reached out and rang a bell. The butler appeared and she called for tea. "Now," Effie ran on, unable to stem the flow now that she finally had a listener, "we shall settle in for a good cose, and you must tell me what Mary and James are up to these days, and your brothers, and, of course, all about your beaux. I wager you have many of them."

Daphne would no sooner answer one question of Mama's activities than three more would be fired at her head. She was a little confused, but happy to see her aunt so alert and talkative. An hour later, with her head in a whirl, Daphne went to her room to relax after her trip, and later to change for dinner.

Aunt Effie had exerted herself to make this first meal a particularly fine one. What silver, crystal, and china she still possessed were all cleaned and polished and laid on the table in a very closet of a dining parlour. The food was good and plentiful, and when Daphne got over the feeling she was eating in a clothespress, she enjoyed it.

"Try this ragout," Effie said, passing along a dish. There was no room for footmen at their elbows, and the niece doubted that such people were on the premises at all. "I got the recipe from Lady Devonshire's Pierre years ago. Lord Holland most particularly liked it."

Later, when dessert wine was poured into her glass, Effie said, "This should be good. It's old enough. It has sat in the cellars since the last century. Fox gave it to me for helping him win the election in '85, I think it was," she added casually.

"Fox, the great statesman?" Daphne asked, feeling that at last she was approaching the *real* Aunt Effie of legend.

"To be sure, my dear. What a treasure he was! When Pitt had the parliament dissolved, you must know, we all—all the Prince of Wales's set—got together and decided dear Charles must be our next prime minister. Prinney was a Whig then, fancy! The ladies took an active part in politics in those days. Georgiana, the Duchess of Devonshire, and I rounded up a bunch of ladies to go down into the most blackguard houses of Long Acres, begging votes and buying them with a kiss when we had to. We all wore a fox brush in our caps, and his buff-and-blue colours in a scarf, and combed his area. And when he won—what a revel! We stayed up all night partying at Devonshire House, and the next day Prinney had a do at Carlton House that lasted from noon till six. I didn't sleep for three days. That same night we went on to Mrs. Crewes for another party. I was married to Lord Standington in those days and moved in the best circles."

"And you actually knew the Prince of Wales personally?" Daphne enquired.

"Knew him! My dear, he spent a week with Standington and myself at Arthur's hunting box in Leicester, with Marie—Mrs. Fitzherbert, you know. Such a sweet thing she was, only quite stout and with rather a long nose, but very sweet. Georgiana told me *such* a story about Marie and the Prince. She was present at their betrothal, I suppose you would call it. The Prince was dying for Marie, and she would have nothing to do with him—he couldn't legally marry her because of the Marriage Act, of course. Her a Papist amongst other things, and a widow! So the Prince had his quack in to leech him—he liked to look pale and romantic. There was a cup of blood drawn, and what must he do but pour it all over himself, cut a hole in his jacket, and send for Marie, pretending he'd tried to commit suicide for love of her. But she wouldn't go to him without a lady escort, and that is how Georgiana came to be in on it. I wish she had called me. He proposed marriage, and Marie accepted—wrote to the Pope and all to see if it would do. Later they had a sort of marriage ceremony, though neither of them ever declared it publicly and later, when they made Prinney marry that horrid Caroline, he just dropped Marie. They may say what they will of a divorcée, at least I'm not a bigamist."

With interesting stories and characters of this sort to beguile the evening, it passed quickly. The ladies went from dining room to Blue Saloon with hardly a gap in the conversation. Tales incredible to believe were unfolded with such a wealth of detail as to name, place and circumstance that there was no disbelieving them. Then, too, despite her eventful life, Effie was not an imaginative person. She was, in fact, that sort of realist who would halt a conversation for five minutes to recall whether it was Mr. Pettigrew or his brother Robert who was second best man at a wedding, when the wedding itself was only a diversion in some other story.

"What a memory you have, Aunt," Daphne complimented her. "And what a lot of interesting stories."

"My memory begins to fail me, dear. I'm not sure yet whether it was Mr. Pettigrew or Robert— but in any case I have been reading those stories over in my memoirs these past months I have been so alone, and that's why they are fresh in mind now."

"Oh, you have kept a diary! What a splendid idea! I used to myself, but it seemed pointless to write each day that I had helped hem up a pair of curtains, or went for a ride in the woods, or drove to the village, so I stopped."

"I shouldn't bother to start till my life got a little more interesting, if I were you, for there's nothing makes one so peevish as reading a book where nothing happens."

"Nothing of the sort you have been describing is likely to happen in my life, Auntie."

"Never say never. It is something I learned long ago. I used to say I'd never hold up my head again when Standington walked out on me, and never be poor again when I married Mr. Eglinton, and never marry again when he died. But all my nevers came back to taunt me, and now I *hardly ever* say it, for I shan't even say I never say never. It is, perhaps, unlikely I shall remarry and be rich again, but there—who is to say? But as to yourself, the case is quite different. You are young and attractive and in London. Oh, I know I can't present you as I should dearly love to do, my dear, but there are gentlemen with eyes in their heads for all that, and I had not been presented yet when Standington saw me, looking in at a shop window, and followed me. He was so clever. He came to the door not five minutes after I got home and said he'd seen me drop a trinket—a watch fob it was— and followed me home to return it. I'd never seen it before in my life. How should I, for he took it from his own chain for the purpose, and it served as an introduction. Before long he was calling every day. What a handsome man he was—so straight and with shoulders as wide as a door." The blue eyes took on their glazed "memory" look.

Daphne was already beginning to have some understanding of her aunt. Of all her husbands, it was only the first who brought this certain smile to her lips. He was the great love of her life—no doubt of that. Her fondest and most frequent memories were of her life in England with him, and they were only married for eighteen months. Even the divorce had not soured those memories. Daphne was curious to have a look at the memoirs. "Did you write that episode up in your memoirs, Aunt? It seems to me from that date on your life was interesting enough to record."

"It was interesting enough a month before that. I started it the day I came to London to visit the Elders. That was their name, not age. Relatives on Papa's side. Yes, there was a very interesting month even before Standington wangled his introduction. You must have a look at my diary one day, if you can read my scratching. I haven't kept it since I married Mr. Pealing, but now that you are come, I think I'll start it again, for with such an attractive young lady in the house, I have a feeling things will pick up. I am very good at *feelings*."

She was off on another tale having to do with a premonition that Lord Alvanley would escape unscathed from a duel with Morgan O'Connell, as indeed he had. "And now I have the feeling that things are going to start to happen again. It's hard to describe what I mean. The blood quickens and there's a feeling of excitement inside my head. Mary would know what I meant. *She* used to get feelings, too."

"I hope you may be right, Ma'am," Daphne said, with the secret thought that her aunt's manifestations of feeling might be due to Mr. Fox's excellent wine.

"Oh, I am never wrong about my feelings."

"What, *never*?" her niece teased.

"Hardly ever," Effie corrected herself, and together they went off to their chambers.

Three

AUNT Effie's premonition of great things about to happen did not come to pass immediately. Nothing occurred during the first three days of the visit. The lavish dinner of the first evening was not repeated, and Daphne soon learned that her aunt kept no carriage. "Actually I have a carriage," Effie told her, "but I don't keep horses. In the first place, they charge extra for the stable that goes with the apartment, and in the second place, it requires a groom and such a ton of feed, for horses do nothing but eat their heads off all the time you're not using them. And I don't go about enough to make it worth my while."

"Then why don't you sell the carriage?" her niece asked.

"Well, it is the carriage Standington gave me for a wedding present, and I wouldn't like to part with it. I had the crest painted over, of course."

Daphne had to repress a sigh at this foolish streak of romanticism. Her aunt obviously needed the money, and she also felt that Effie would hire a team for the months of her visit if she could afford it. The quality of the wine had been inferior after the first night, and the general state of creeping decay in all the furnishings, such as drapes and carpets, was further evidence of a lack of funds.

One day Daphne found her aunt in a little study—the one which held the memoirs, often dipped into to pass the time. She was frowning over a fistful of bills and shaking her head. "Bills," she said in accents of loathing. "I'm sure I don't know how I managed to eat up five guineas worth of meat in a month, but here is the bill from the butcher, and Cook confirms it. And look at this, Daphne, three guineas for candles, in spite of using tallow ones in the kitchen. I certainly didn't used to spend so much for candles. And here are more bills just come. I don't believe I'll bother to open them." Setting the bills aside she went on, "I'm sure they're making the days shorter."

"That one doesn't look like a bill," Daphne said, pointing out an envelope of a superior quality.

Effie eyed it suspiciously, but at last opened it and pulled out a letter. "It's from a Mr. Henry Colburn," she said. "I never heard of him. Who can he be?"

"Read the letter and find out," she was advised.

"Good gracious me! Was there ever such nonsense? He wants me to write a book," she said, laughing.

This sounded such a bizarre request to come out of the blue that Daphne reached out her hand for the letter. It sounded less bizarre after she read the letter's contents. Mr. Colburn knew Aunt Effie's history and had suggested she write her reminiscences of the great people she had known. He mentioned her travels abroad, which were of interest to those who stayed at home. "It's a stunning idea!" Daphne said, thinking of the revenue that might come from such a book. She also saw the editing of the memoirs as a useful and amusing occupation after she returned home and her aunt would be again alone. Effie would meet some new friends, have somewhere to go and someone to visit her.

"It is not to be thought of," the aunt said, setting the letter aside with the bills. "I'm sure I would never sink so low."

"There is that *never* again!" Daphne roasted. "It is not in the least low, Ma'am. Many of your reminiscences are unexceptionable. They show no one in a poor light. Your soliciting votes for Fox, for instance, would harm no one and be of interest to many. Your experience in France where you lost your diamond necklace and it turned up next day in the pot-au-feu, too, was most unusual and amusing. You would not, of course, put in those sections where certain people took advantage of you. No need to tell how many you helped with money only to be spurned when they were in a position to return the favour; and, of course, it wouldn't do to brag how you had to fight off the men with a sledge hammer."

"But if it is announced that *I* am to write a book, people will expect to read about—you know, the divorce and all that. I would never—there I go again—but I never would write a word about that, and that is what people would expect: Scandal."

"Let them think what they like, Auntie, if it will make them buy the book. You needn't fulfill their lurid expectations. Write about what you wish. There is enough material in your diaries to write a good long book without resorting to any shameful revelations to yourself or anyone else."

"James wouldn't like it," was the answer.

"James who?" Daphne asked, trying to recall if James was one of the husbands.

"Your father," Effie replied, startled. "You know what a demon for propriety he is. Methodist. Why, he won't let Mary walk in the village without an abigail to this day. He wouldn't care for it at all."

"Aunt Effie! My father may go to the devil. This has nothing to do with him. Mama knuckles under to him too easily nine times out of ten. If he were my *husband* instead of father he wouldn't be so overbearing. As he does not see fit to ask you to come to us, as he should do, you need not consider what he will think. Anyway, it isn't nearly so dashing as some of the other things you've done."

"Well, Arthur wouldn't care for it either."

"Pooh! I don't suppose *you* much cared to be divorced. He could have made it a separation, as he didn't wish to remarry, and saved you a lot of disgrace."

"But then I could never have married Mr. Eglinton, and, really, he was quite amusing, too, though not the fine figure of a man Arthur was. But there is another problem as well. I have no style for writing. I just jotted my notes down any old higgledy-piggledy way. You know what a mess they are. I can't spell, and never know where to put semi-colons and all those dots and dashes real

writers use. I always found writing very confus-
ing."

"Mr. Colburn must have some sort of a person
who will dot the 'i's and cross the 't's."

"Oh well, I can do that much myself."

"Aunt Effie, you goose! I didn't mean... But
never mind. I am fairly good at a semi-colon myself
and will give you a hand while I am here. We have
nothing else to do. It will be great fun."

"What a flat time I am showing you, when you
are ready to tackle writing to get the days in."

"No, I didn't mean that. Oh, do it! You had the
feeling something was going to happen, and this is
the first thing that has promised any excitement."

"Well," Effie said, considering the matter. "I'll
just write Mr. Colburn a little note asking if he
would care to drop around and discuss it. I'll let
him know what kind of a book we have in mind,
and if he isn't interested in that, I shan't do it. You
must help me with the note, Daphne. Put in some of
those semi-colons, and a few commas, too, so he
won't think I'm illiterate."

The note was written with pertinent punctuation, Mr. Colburn came two days later, and it was
very pleasant to at last have a caller. He was a
small, dandified gentleman with pink cheeks and
a fringe of brindled hair. He took to Effie
immediately and she liked him also, having been
deprived of all masculine company but servants
for a year. In fact, he stayed so long Daphne began
to wonder whether there wasn't some romance in
the air. But his main concern was to urge a little
livelier story on Mrs. Pealing than she intended.
He did not insist on any record of the divorce,
however, and before he left they had come to an

understanding that she would begin her book immediately, to be ready for publication within the year.

Mr. Colburn intended to pay many calls at Upper Grosvenor Square and lure the unsuspecting lady into greater revelations than she had any intention of making. She couldn't be as straight-laced about her past as she let on. And there might be a bit of lovemaking to be done as well, in the way of business and pleasure. With luck, he'd get a hand on those memoirs himself and do a proper job once she came to trust him.

Through a friend in the newspaper business he managed to get an article inserted in a social column mentioning that Mrs. Pealing, with all her other names, was to publish her memoirs. Neither Mrs. Pealing nor Daphne Ingleside saw the notice, but it was read by those whose chief literature was the social columns and received with joy or dismay, depending on past dealings with the author.

A certain Lady Elizabeth Thyrwite read it and turned pale. "That woman! I hoped—thought she was dead!" she said to herself and dropped the paper to the floor, trembling. Her husband, Sir Lawrence Thyrwite, was a Member of Parliament and making great strides in his career. After having sat with the Tories for twenty years, speaking in the House three times, and never voting against his party, he was in line for promotion. He was a pillar of rectitude, his one lapse from virtue having occurred the year before their marriage, when he, in common with every other gentleman in London at the time, had thrown his heart at Mrs. Pealing's (then the widowed Mrs. Eglinton's) feet. It was being discussed that he was to be given a folio in the Cabinet. It was within an inch of his grasp, and now this! If that woman published how Larry had begged her to marry him, had broken his engagement to a Miss Marmon, a stupid little chit who had only ever got hold of him by letting on that she was related to the Sussex Marmons (and it was no such a thing)—if she told the world how he had a ring-round fight with his family, and threatened to renounce his inheritance, he would be ruined! Such unwise, unpolitical, unministerial behaviour! All that was past and forgotten when he had had the good taste and luck to fall in love with herself, after being turned down by Mrs. Eglinton. Not a whisper of an opera dancer or an actress had sullied his name from that moment on, and it was too bad for a Mrs. Pealing to ruin a man's life for cheap sensationalism and a bit of money. She must be stopped, and Sir Lawrence must not go near her to do it, for he still had a loose-lipped smile on those rare occasions when her name arose. Dickie, Lady Elizabeth's brother, must be sent as emissary to buy off the hussy. Lawrence must not hear a word of it. If anyone mentioned the matter to him, he would be met with innocent looks; Larry was such a ninny he would be only surprised and not shaking in his boots as he ought to be, for he still claimed that Effie had a heart of gold and wouldn't harm a fly.

Dickie was quite a different matter. Though he was only a younger brother, he was wide awake on all suits. No one would pull a trick on Richard. Lady Elizabeth was accustomed to apply to him in all her various difficulties, and he had never let her down yet. Whether it was getting a job for Larry's brother or a ticket for a play when she had cancelled her box for the Season or a safe seat in Parliament for Larry when his own was in jeopardy, Dickie always came through. He was very tyrannical, of course, and insisted that you follow his orders to the letter; but, really, he was very efficient and exactly the right person to handle this touchy business. He would certainly be ready to help on this occasion, for he had the greatest dislike of low persons who would spread gossip. He was very proper in all of his dealings and very discreet in those that weren't so proper. As the nephew of the Archbishop of Canterbury— Mama's brother—he was aware that propriety was expected of him. He could be taken as a model of decorous behaviour.

Richard Percival, the Duke of St. Felix, duly received a hastily scribbled note from his sister requesting his immediate attendance on her. Accustomed to the minor matters that Bess considered urgent, he tossed the note on a table and reminded himself to drop in the next day. In other households, similar plans were afoot to drop in on Mrs. Pealing, who sat all unaware, smiling over her memoirs and reading aloud a paragraph here and there to Daphne, who was busy with a pencil ticking off likely items for inclusion in the book. At eleven they retired and had the last night of easy sleep either was to have for the next several weeks.

Their door knocker started banging early the next day. Who should drop in but Lady Pamela Thurston of the pawned diamonds. Effie hadn't seen her in over twenty years but recognized her at once. Lady Pamela's face had sagged half an inch, but the hair was the same insouciant shade of pinkish-orange, achieved with the same dye that had first wrought the minor miracle a quarter of a century before. There was no one else in London with hair the shade of Pamela's.

"Pamela Thurston, I declare!" Effie exclaimed, and her blue eyes opened wide in shock. "Where have *you* come from after all these years?"

"Effie, is it *you!*" Lady Pamela asked. The blue hair was not so easily recognized, nor the full pink cheeks. The surroundings were so altogether different from what Mrs. Eglinton used to enjoy. The carpet underfoot was positively thread-bare and the drapes tatty. All was seen in one room-encircling gaze, then the eyes went back to Mrs. Pealing.

"To be sure it is. Wouldn't you have known me, Pamela?"

"I would have known *her!*" Lady Pamela replied, pointing to Daphne, and then she laughed, a deep, throaty gurgle. How good it was to hear the sound of laughter again. "The spit and image of you, Effie. I had no idea you had a daughter."

"This is my niece," Effie said, and made the introduction.

Daphne realized she was in the presence of a life previously unknown to her. The hair, the furs, the perfume, the polish—all were new. Wealth and self-confidence exuded from Lady Pamela. Here at last was a creature from the enchanted kingdom of Aunt Effie-land, and Daphne waited with baited breath to hear her speak on. All that she heard was a great deal of senseless chatter of "Do you remember?" this one and that one. She was disappointed, but at length some sense began to emerge from the chatter. "And I said to Sammie when I saw the notice in the *Observer*—you remember my darling Sammie—'Effie Eglinton! Why, I didn't know she was still in London! I must pay her a call.' And then I remembered—dear Effie, you must think me the most mindless person the good Lord ever created, but not till that very instant did I remember your having got my diamond necklace back from the pawn shop for me twenty-five years ago. I never paid you back a penny. Five hundred pounds, wasn't it?"

"I do believe it was. Yes, five hundred wasn't it, Daphne? We were reading of it in my memoirs last night," Effie said.

Lady Pamela shot a sharp look through narrowed eyes at dear Mrs. Pealing.

"Yes, five hundred pounds twenty-five years ago, when it was worth so much more," Daphne replied, smiling as sweetly as their caller.

"And interest, of course, at five percent, just like in the funds," Pamela returned. "Well, I'll make it twelve hundred pounds, love. Will that do?" She scribbled out a cheque as she spoke.

"Oh my, I never thought to see a penny of it," Effie said happily.

"And it won't be mentioned in the book you're writing, Effie? Sammie never did know about that year I lost all the money gambling, and I managed to save back every penny of it." A good many other things Sammie didn't know remained unmentioned, for Lady Pamela was not sure Mrs. Pealing knew of them either. "Do you remember how Georgiana was always losing at loo?" she laughed.

"Why, Pamela, it's not that kind of a book," Effie said on the brink of offence. "I wouldn't mention dear Georgiana, and she in her grave."

"Oh, no, I'm sure it's not, but you won't mention me all the same?"

"What is there to mention?" Effie replied in mindless delight as the cheque was handed over to her. "You don't owe me anything *now*, Pamela. We're even, so let's forget it. Have a glass of wine."

The glass of wine was drunk up with a haste not usually achieved on a morning visit; and with a great sigh of relief, Lady Pamela was off to report to a few worried friends that Effie was very manageable, but you had to pay up with interest. Lady Pamela's friends consulted their bank books and investments and sat down to compute interest for twenty-five years at five percent.

"What did that lady mean, she saw the notice in the *Observer*?" Daphne asked after she had admired the cheque.

"What notice? She didn't mention anything about a notice," Effie answered.

Daphne had already perceived that her aunt was not quite as bright as she might be and went off to peruse the *Observer* for the notice. After much searching she found the note in the social column and fell to wondering. Lady Pamela had been worried and had made a point of not having her debt mentioned. She had come here to pay so Auntie wouldn't mention it in her book, Daphne soon deduced. What a horrid mind!

While she was finishing her conjecture, there was another caller announced and a Major Deitweiller came in. After the merest mention of surprise at seeing Effie's name in the paper after so many years, his business, too, soon emerged. He owed her a thousand pounds for the purchase of his commission in the Army and now, as a respectable, well-to-do major, he wished to repay the loan. He did not mention interest, nor did Daphne nor Effie. He paid a thousand in cash and left very soon afterwards, with the casual mention that he supposed her having helped him all those years ago would not be in the book. His wife—he had married a Miss Norton from Warwick, one of *the* Nortons—didn't know of his lowly beginnings, he laughed nervously.

"Oh, no, it is more of a book of travel," Effie smiled. "Though, as I have been looking through my memoirs these past days, a good many stories from London occur to me that might make interesting reading. Do you remember, Major, that young Harcourt fellow who used to chum around with you? He joined up at the same time as yourself." He had also joined up through the same financial arrangement as Deitweiller, though it was not said. "He was dangling after Lord Severn's girl and had a pretty little actress on the side."

"Yes, I see him often," Deitweiller said. "He plans to come to call on you shortly, Ma'am."

"That's good. I look forward to seeing him."

"I'll tell him, Mrs. Pealing. Good day." Harcourt was informed of the matter, and sold his team of greys and his wife's pearls to raise the wind.

"He was in a bit of a hurry," Effie said to her niece. "I was just going to remind him of the night

Harcourt rode his horse up the front steps and into my hallway, but I suppose I shouldn't relate such a story as that in the book. He is a Colonel now, and stands very high on his dignity, I daresay. Funny to think of all those young bucks having risen so high in the world and not a brain to speak of among the lot of them."

Before they sat down to lunch they had a third caller—a Mr. Munro—coming to repay Effie a debt of two hundred pounds for some matter she had forgotten long since and was sure she had not bothered to record in her memoirs. She remembered Munro, but not why he insisted he owed her two hundred pounds. "Was there ever such a thing, Daphne?" she chirped merrily. "Twenty-four hundred pounds in one morning coming at us out of the blue. All my old friends remembering me and coming to pay what they owe. None of them knew where I was living, and that is why they haven't been to call sooner. It was that notice in the paper that has brought them back to me. How happy I am I decided to write it after all. Didn't I *tell* you I had a feeling things would happen? My feelings are never wrong. It's a fact. I am not clever, but I feel things before they happen."

"Do you think it is just friendship that brings them back?" Daphne asked. Her own opinion was growing stronger with each visit that it was fear of revelation in the book that brought them.

"What else could it be, my dear?"

Daphne mentioned her own opinion and was talked down as being suspicious and mean-natured, "which you get from James, dear, and nothing can be done about it; but I do wish you would not take that notion into your head or you will spoil all our fun."

"I could be wrong. They're your friends, and you must know them better than I."

"I should say I do, and they are not at all like that, Daphne, so pray banish the thought."

"It is banished," Daphne told her, not quite truthfully. "And what do those intriguing feelings of yours inform you we have in store for this afternoon?"

Effie shivered. "How strange," she said. "A chill just ran over me. I got the feeling someone..."

"An *evil person*?" Daphne asked quizzingly.

"No, not evil precisely. More troublesome," Effie said.

"It will be interesting to see who else has read the *Observer*," Daphne answered, and ate her omelette without paying the least heed to Effie's warning, which was rather a pity. But then the six-feet-and-two-inches of trouble that was on its way would not have been turned aside in any case, for when the Duke of St. Felix undertook to do a thing, he did it thoroughly.

Four

THE day after receiving his sister's summons to Charles Street, St. Felix stopped by to see what old Bess was in a pucker about now. The late Duke of St. Felix had fathered four children, each spaced five years apart. He had not hurried his breeding. The eldest, Elizabeth, was forty-five; the other two daughters forty and thirty-five; with Richard, the precious son and heir, a mere stripling of thirty in this family of aging women. Despite his youth, he ruled the family as firmly as ever his father had done. From his sire he had come to appreciate the value of the perquisites that were his to bestow, and none were bestowed on those who failed to live up to his high standards. He was generous to the brink of fault with relatives whose sons did well at Oxford and distinguished themselves in those jobs he found for them; but let a daughter make a poor

35

match or behave in any unseemly manner and she was called severely to account. He did not despise liveliness or spirit in the extended family over which he held sway, but the semblance of propriety was always to be maintained. He spoke a good deal of the family's name and reputation, as though they were living things, subject to physical deterioration.

Elizabeth was awaiting her brother in her Gold Saloon, hoping to soften him with a glass of Larry's very best burgundy.

"Good afternoon, Bess," he said with a smile. It cheered him to see his sisters living in good, respectable homes surrounded by luxury and tokens of success. He was particularly close to Lady Thyrwite, as she was the only one of his sisters to reside in London, like himself. The others were well married into influential county families and received semi-annual visits from their brother to see that they were not slipping into obscurity or any other bad habits.

"Dickie!" Bess began, and at the one word his genial smile faded.

"I have been asking you for twenty years to call me Richard," he said. It seemed a reasonable request from a very tall gentleman in his thirty-first year.

"Sorry, Richard, but it slipped out. I still think of you as my dear little brother."

"What can I do for you?"

She indicated a chair and poured him a glass of wine. She was tempted to invite him to have a cheroot, for she wished him to be in a good mood, but then the stench lingered so, like burning garbage. "I want to ask you to do a little favour for me, Richard."

"So I assumed. What is it?"

She cleared her throat. "I wonder if you would be kind enough to drop by Mrs. Pealing's place for me, and ..."

"Who the devil is Mrs. Pealing?"

"You can't mean you don't know of Mrs. Pealing, the ex-Countess Standington!"

"Oh—also ex-Mrs. something else, isn't she? I heard some mention of her yesterday. Writing a book of reminiscences, I believe. Is that the one?" Bess nodded. "She seems to have the whole town in a twitter with this book of hers."

"Yes," she said grimly.

"Now why in the world should I call on her? She is exactly the sort of person I abhor. To live a life of debauchery and then, in her old age, to make public her conquests. What do you have to do with the woman?"

"Nothing. I don't know her at all."

"I shouldn't think you'd want to."

"I don't, but the thing is ... It's this book she's writing."

Richard stared in fascination, a slow smile spreading across his handsome face. "You don't mean to say *you* ever performed an act worthy of publication in the book, Bess?" he asked.

"Certainly not! It is no such a thing."

"Ah—you blast my hopes. I had thought there for a moment that in your salad days you had cut up a lark. It's Larry, then, is it?"

"Yes, and she must be bought off, Dickie— Richard!"

"What did he do?"

St. Felix was treated to an expurgated, white-washed, and harmless version of the straying of Lawrence, and lifted a brow in question. "It'll hardly set the town on its ear that he once paid a few calls to Mrs. Pealing," he pointed out.

"It was more than that." The story came out in bits and pieces, until after fifteen minutes St. Felix was more or less possessed of the facts and reminded that a folio in the Cabinet hung in the balance—a fine ornament for the family's reputation.

"Very well, I'll go with Larry," he decided. "I confess I am curious to see the latest scandal. And I'd better make sure he don't overpay. Not a penny more than five hundred pounds in my opinion. If I have the *whole story*, that is," he finished up.

This jibe went unanswered. "No, Richard, Larry must not go with you. I want you to go for him. You deal with her, you are better able to handle *her* sort."

"On what do you base that opinion?" he asked.

"Oh mercy, Dickie, don't get satirical on me. I am desperate! You know Larry's a fool—that is . . . I don't mean—only he is not shrewd like you and not able to give a set-down half so well."

"Thank you," Richard said in a thin voice. "Tell me, is Larry to foot the bill at least, or am I to have that honour, as well?"

"I took a thousand pounds from the bank. I hope she'll settle for five hundred."

"She will," Richard said, arising.

"Lady Pamela Thurston stopped by for lunch.

She went to pay up yesterday, and she says they are demanding interest."

"I don't know why you associate with that creature. Hair the colour of a flamingo." He stopped in mid-tirade. "Did you say *they*? Is Pealing in on it, as well? I thought I heard she was a widow."

"She is, but she has a girl staying with her. A niece, I believe; and Lady Pamela says she's the image of Mrs. Pealing at the same age. She was very pretty, you know."

"I didn't suppose an antidote had half of London at her feet," he said, continuing towards the door.

"Come right back and let me know!" Bess called after him and then took up her vigil.

St. Felix drove his curricle to Upper Grosvenor Square and eyed a somewhat ramshackle apartment building with scorn. What a fool old Mrs. Pealing must be to have run through the fortune Eglinton left her and be living in such squalor as this. He gave his card to the butler and said he had come on a matter of business.

The card was handed to Mrs. Pealing, who sat in the study with Miss Ingleside, continuing on the work of editing. Her pink face paled, and she said, "Impossible! He's dead."

"Who is dead?" Daphne asked.

"St. Felix."

"Oh yes, for a certainty. They never canonize a living person. But who on earth—or in heaven—is St. Felix?"

Effie handed her the card. "Oh, the *Duke* of St.

Felix," Daphne smiled, impressed. A baronet's wife and a colonel were their lordliest callers thus far. "I wonder how much gold is jingling in *his* pockets. We'd better go in and see him."

"Not I!" Effie stated firmly. "I am too busy."

"Auntie, you can't leave a *duke* cooling his heels. Now do use your head. It isn't the dead St. Felix flitted down from heaven to see you. It is his heir, probably his son. Come along. I'll go with you."

"No, no. I do not wish at all to see St. Felix. Perhaps you could handle it, dear."

Sensing a heavy windfall from a long overdue debt to be waiting in the next room, Daphne was not inclined to lose it only because her aunt was suddenly shy of this man she had never met. "Very well, I'll see him. But before I go, what was the nature of the other St. Felix's dealings with you?"

"We were—just friends," she answered vaguely.

"Did you lend him money?"

"Lend St. Felix money? Lord, no, he had more of it than I."

"I see," Daphne replied, surprised. Was it possible one person was actually calling out of mere friendship?

When she was face to face with St. Felix, she relinquished the thought. There was no token of friendship on the formidable gentleman's arrogant face, nor indication of it in his stiff bearing.

"Miss Pealing?" he asked, looking her over from head to toe with cold grey eyes.

She returned the inspection, taking in a well-cut coat of blue Bath cloth, an elegant but unexaggerated cravat, a generally subdued outfit. He was too tall for the foppish mode. "Miss Ingleside. I am Mrs. Pealing's niece. She is indisposed and asked me to see you in her stead. Pray be seated, Your Grace."

He sat, still regarding her coldly. "I daresay you are privy to her dealings, and we can handle the matter between us."

"Very likely. What is your business with my aunt?"

"*I* have no business with her, I am happy to say. I am here on behalf of Sir Lawrence Thyrwite."

The name conveyed nothing to Miss Ingleside. She had not read all the memoirs, by any means. "And what is Sir Lawrence's business with my aunt? I am sorry, I know nothing of him."

"His business at the moment is of only a financial nature. There is no need to go into details. Just tell me the sum."

"Oh, he owes her money, you mean?" she asked, smiling with satisfaction. At this rate, the book would bring in more before its publication than it was likely to do after.

"That is a matter of opinion. He is willing to pay in any case."

"I'm sure we don't want him to pay if he didn't borrow anything," she said, disliking the tone of her caller. The others had at least put a decent face on it—pretended friendship. "We are not extortionists, you know."

"How much are you charging for your silence?" he asked in a sneering voice.

"I told you we are not extortionists! If Sir Lawrence owes nothing, certainly we want nothing from him."

"I would prefer not to have to return to this place," he stated with an emphasis that implied the "place" was a snakepit. "What is the price?"

"Well, 'Silence is Golden', you know," she answered, piqued into ill humour herself.

"Will five hundred do it?"

"I had best speak to my aunt. Perhaps she recalls Sir Lawrence." She left and walked at a sedate pace till she was beyond his view; then she broke into a run.

"Auntie, who on earth is Sir Lawrence Thyrwite?" she asked, breathless.

"Larry Thyrwite? Gracious, I haven't thought of that ninny in a quarter of a century. Is he here?"

"No, St. Felix is here on his behalf. Does this Sir Lawrence owe you money?"

"No, I never gave him anything. He used to try to make love to me after Jerry died, but I didn't care for his lips. They hung open in that loose way some dull-witted people have. He is married now to—oh, dear!—St. Felix's daughter. That is why that man is here."

"Daughter! He can't be more than... Oh, married to the sister of this St. Felix, I suppose. And you are sure you didn't lend him any money? Think hard, Auntie. He mentioned five hundred pounds, and I would dearly love to gouge this gentleman."

"It doesn't need thinking about. Larry was always well to grass. He only came around for romance and didn't get much of it, either."

"Too bad. I'll send St. Felix off then." She was extremely sorry to have to let him off so easily.

"There seems to be some misunderstanding,"

Daphne said to St. Felix when she returned to the Blue Saloon. "My aunt finds Sir Lawrence owes her no money."

Richard regarded her closely, and considered this statement carefully. "Owes her no *money*"— what did that imply?

"They were just friends, you see," Daphne went on, feeling uncomfortable in a totally silent room with those probing eyes staring through her. "In common with the rest of my aunt's ex-friends, he has not been to see her for many years." He continued to listen and think and stare, and she became increasingly angry at his silence.

"It is really quite shocking the way everyone has deserted my aunt. When I came here, she hadn't had a single caller in a month. People only used her, took advantage of her generosity when she lived on Half Moon Street; and now that she is getting on and is poor, no one comes near her."

Richard thought he had her meaning now. Mrs. Pealing wished to re-enter Society. "Where do *you* come into it?" he asked.

"I? I don't come into it at all. I am her niece. I happen to be visiting her, that's all."

"Are you to make your debut this Season?"

"No, my aunt is in no position to sponsor me. It is only a family visit, and a quite dull one it has been, too."

"She would wish to show you a livelier time, I assume?"

"I'm sure she would, if it were possible. She used to be very sociable, some years ago."

"I shouldn't think it would be at all possible, the way you are going about it. You are more likely to alienate your aunt's former friends than endear yourself to them by blackmail."

"Blackmail?" she said, not entirely surprised at the charge but angry nevertheless. "We have not threatened nor intimidated anyone, nor done anything illegal. My aunt has merely announced that she is going to publish a few memoirs from her youth."

"It is tantamount to blackmail to threaten to publish licentious stories and accept payment for *not* publishing them."

"Yes, certainly it is, but we are not doing anything of the kind. If people who sponged off my aunt when she was rich have been goaded into repaying their lawful debts to her only because they are so mean-minded they think she intends to expose them in her book, well, it is no more than is her due!"

"It won't work," he said and arose from his chair, to tower over her.

"Will it not? We'll see about that, Your Grace. It has already worked. She has had over twenty-four hundred pounds repaid already, every cent of it coming to her honestly."

"Yes, with interest, I hear. You'll find money alone opens no doors. She may bleed people white, but she won't be invited back into Society. There is some behaviour that puts one beyond the pale of decent society. Divorce and blackmail, for example."

"She isn't bleeding anyone! They owe her the money, and why should they not pay interest? They have been getting five percent in the funds.

Why should my aunt's investments pay no interest?"

"Why settle for five percent? The usurers charge fifty. There is a good business tip for you, Miss. Put your ill-got gains out to loan at exorbitant interest rates and you'll achieve your end sooner. You'll be rich enough for anything, except common decency."

"Thank you for the advice, Your Grace. I shall be sure to tell where it came from, if I decide to take your advice. Is that how you manage to present so affluent an appearance?"

"Oh, no, *I* am a gentleman. I merely suggested a notion that I thought might appeal to *you.* I wish you luck, Ma'am, and look forward to reading an interesting chapter on the amorous exploits of Sir Lawrence, for you'll find no interest has accrued to you in that quarter."

"There will be no amorous exploits regarding Sir Lawrence. My aunt said he *tried* to make love to her, but she took an aversion to his open mouth. She could not like the dull-witted appearance it gave him. You may read *that* in the book, but you can assure your sister we don't plan to allege any affair with so unattractive a person. We mean to retain some shred of dignity, you see."

"You have had time to discover my relationship with Sir Lawrence already? You run an efficient operation. I hope you have taken the precaution of hiring yourself a sharp solicitor. You'll be hearing from Sir Lawrence's. I would advise you not to print anything of the sort you mentioned if you don't wish to be charged with a libel suit."

"Something must be untrue to be libelous, if I am not mistaken, and the world can see for itself that Sir Lawrence has loose lips," she flung back.

"I suggest you consult your attorney on the subject of detraction."

"We don't have an attorney."

"High time you hired one. Good day, Ma'am." He strode angrily from the room and went straight back to Bess to open his budget.

"They aren't after money," he said. "They're getting that, apparently, from people who actually owe the old girl something. What they want from you and others of our sort is the entrée to Society."

"Oh, Dickie, you've made a botch of it!" Bess moaned. "I cannot ask that woman here. I'd be the laughing stock of the world. Everyone is talking about her."

"I don't propose you should ask her. I haven't taken leave of my senses."

"What will they do if I don't?"

"Put Larry into the book, describing in detail, no doubt, how he used to make a puppy of himself dangling after the Pealing. All that old business of his ditching the Marmon girl will be raked up as a result. Yes, and they mean to add a few paragraphs on the condition of his lips, too, I believe."

"Oh, my God! Pay them. Give them whatever sum it takes. This will ruin his chances for advancement. Go back and take them the whole thousand."

"I have done better. I am going to have my solicitor see them. Scare them off with the threat of a libel suit."

"What's that?"

"It happens to be against the law to defame anyone's character. Malicious misrepresentations..."

"Yes, Dickie, but it isn't *mis*representation. He *did* dangle after her."

"Well, detraction then, if it's a criminal offence. There must be some legal trick Willoughby can use. I don't see why you should give them any money, and I certainly do not advise you to invite them to your home."

"Never in the world. That is definitely not to be considered."

"I'll send Willoughby around to put a scare into them. They don't have a lawyer. They are just amateurs."

"No, don't do that. It will show them we take it too seriously, and will antagonize them too. Offer them money. Enough to keep the woman still."

"Not one red penny."

"A thousand pounds. I can spare it, and the promotion is worth a good deal more than that. Larry has waited twenty years for it."

"It wouldn't satisfy her."

"It galls me to have to pay that woman, but... How does she look nowadays, by the way?"

"Who, Mrs. Pealing? I didn't see her. I dealt with the niece."

"Oh. Pamela said she is fat as a flawn and had her hair dyed blue. How vulgar. What is the niece like?"

"As bold as brass."

"Yes, but what does she look like? They say Effie used to look like her years ago. Is she very pretty?"

47

"More beautiful than pretty," he confessed reluctantly.

"Pamela didn't say she was beautiful. Dark hair, I think?"

"Yes, black as coal. A tall girl."

Bess knew her brother to prefer tall girls, being so tall himself. Anything under five feet five inches he described as squat. "What about the face? Come now, draw me a picture of her."

"I didn't pay much attention," he said, but still a vivid image of her lurked inside his head. Grey eyes, long lashes, a strong chin, clear complexion.

"Well, when you go back to give them the money, take a good look."

"I'm not going back."

"You must. Larry can't handle it in his position."

"Write her a letter and enclose a cheque, if you insist on throwing your blunt away. If you don't mean to follow my advice, I don't see why you bother me with your problems."

"Yes, I know you like to have it all your own way, dear, but still I don't want to resort to an attorney."

"Then you have the choice of paying through the nose or having them here."

"I'll write the letter. I can't have them here."

"Let me know what they answer. We must get this business straightened out. As well as Larry's promotion hanging fire, there is Mama's brother about to retire from the archbishopric with an unblemished, indeed an excellent, record of achievement. We don't need any scandal in the family. We have never had it, and it would be a shame if it should come to us through your husband."

"Well *you* are the one who chose him for me, Richard."

"*I* chose him? I was in shortcoats when you married, Bess."

"Oh, my goodness, what made me say that? You looked so very like Papa just now, St. Felix."

St. Felix was insensibly pleased with this comparison. He did not consciously pattern himself after his father, perhaps, but had he been asked to choose the gentleman he most admired in the world, it might well have been his father. He knew he did not live up to that hero's high standards—they were the reach beyond the grasp.

At Upper Grosvenor Square, Daphne ran to her aunt the minute St. Felix left the house. Her intention was to tell her the whole disagreeable conversation, but she was diverted by a question.

"What was St. Felix like?"

"Very tall, and very arrogant."

"His father was tall, too, but never arrogant with me."

"What was your connection with the father? Another suitor?"

"Oh, no, he was married at the time. He was quite a bit older than I."

The dreamy blue eyes belied the denial of romance. "Come now, confess he was in love with you."

"He may have been, a little, but nothing came of it."

"When was this, Auntie?" Daphne asked, intending to do a little reading in the pertinent section of the memoirs to satisfy herself.

"Years ago, in 1785, it was, in the Fall."

This precise recall of the date and season increased Daphne's suspicions, and she intended to follow it up as soon as possible. "Well, whatever about the father, I do not care for the son. He was quite rude."

"Really, what did he say?"

It proved impossible to burden her smiling aunt with the whole story, and she said, "He came to offer you money not to mention Sir Lawrence in your book."

"What nonsense! As if I'd admit to a soul that that ninny ever was sweet on me. I'd pay to keep it a secret. An admirer of his sort adds nothing to one's reputation."

"But what I said before is true, Auntie. These people are coming only for fear of what you will write about them."

"I can't believe that. Lady Pamela was always a good friend, and Major Deitweiller, too, was quite charming."

"Yes, but if they are coming as friends, why do they all shove money at you?"

"Well, my dear, they do *owe* me money, and they must see I am not so high in the stirrups as I was used to be. That is what friends are for, to help one when she is down. Repaying a favour—there is no harm in that."

"No, there is nothing wrong in it; but still we are being taken for a pair of blackmailers."

Aunt Effie laughed merrily at this comment. It was typical of Sir James Ingleside to look for trouble when there was none, of course, and there was no denying Daphne had something of her father in her. Effie returned to her memoirs, to be disturbed very shortly by a Mrs. Acres, come with her fists full of bills, to enquire how the book went on and to repay dear Effie for that money she had lent her for a little holiday in France when she had been feeling poorly, just after her first husband died. And there was no need to mention in the book that Sir Alfred Dwyer had been in France at the time, was there? Lady Dwyer was not at all understanding, to say nothing of Mr. Acres. It was futile to say once again it was not *that* kind of a book. The word was out that it *was* that kind, and the money poured in to buy Mrs. Pealing's silence.

Five

T HE windfall of what now amounted to close
to five thousand pounds was soon being done with
what Effie considered money ought to be done
with—spent. Horses were hired to pull the carriage
and, with an easy conveyance available, the ladies
naturally took to the roads. Daphne must be
shown the Standington mansion on the corner of
Half Moon Street and Piccadilly, the Eglinton
mansion a block up the street, and various other
mansions where Effie had once been accepted and
entertained. The young lady expressed no interest
in the St. Felix mansion, and the aunt did not offer
to point it out. After their tour they went to Bond
Street to peruse the shops. Every ell of blue
material drew Aunt Effie's attention, and before
they went home several had been purchased. In
vain did Miss Ingleside hint at the efficacy of

putting something aside for a rainy day. She was just being James's daughter and as such was not heeded in the least. This foray into the world was taken as a hint by the tardy debtors to pay up, and they came in an ever-increasing stream to renew acquaintance with Mrs. Pealing and to shower her with gold. She had a box of it in her room—many avoided cheques—and was soon calling in a decorator to tear down the drapes, lift up the carpets, recover the sofa and chairs and find new lamps.

One cheque, however, caused some little consternation. "Here is a cheque for one thousand pounds from Lady Elizabeth," Effie said.

"The price has doubled," Daphne replied. "St. Felix mentioned five hundred. Now what can it mean?"

"I told you Larry owes me nothing."

"And I told *you* St. Felix thinks we are blackmailing people."

"Oh, my dear, and St. Felix of all people! I would not have *him* think ill of us."

"What is so special about him?"

"His father was a very dear friend. I told you, Daphne."

"Your eyes tell me he was a good deal more. Come now, Auntie, cut line and tell me the whole of it, if you please." The diaries had contained a good many references to St. Felix, and later, George, who were one and the same, but they had been couched in an unaccustomed discreetness. "George came this evening," for instance, occurred frequently, and on those evenings there seemed to be no other callers admitted, which was unusual, but two of the diary pages had been ripped out. The jagged edge and lapse of time in the Fall of 1785 held a promise of some great happening, but Effie was an oyster on the subject.

"There is nothing to tell. Just friends. But what shall I do with the cheque?"

"Return it. Then he will see we are not blackmailing anyone."

"I can't write to her."

"It is a strange way to treat a dear old friend's children—to avoid them as though they were the plague."

"He was so very nice, Daphne. I hate to think of his children having such a low opinion of me. You write a little note, will you, dear, with some of those punctuation marks you do so well, and I'll sign it."

"Very well, I shall."

The note was written, the cheque enclosed and received as a threatening letter the next day at Charles Street, where Lady Elizabeth went into a fit of strong hysterics and sent for her brother to come at once.

On this occasion, he answered the summons promptly. "They have sent it back," Bess moaned, waving the cheque under Richard's nose.

He scanned the elegantly phrased little note and rightly imagined the hand of Miss Ingleside in the reference to "a mistake in your accounting." "They're holding out for an invitation to the house," Richard declared. "Don't do it, Bess. Don't let our family be the one to let that pair get a toe into the door of Society."

"Yes, but what if they put Larry into their book? The whole town will read how he made a fool of himself over her."

Richard felt this was the lesser of the two evils to be mentioned. There was something degrading about having one's physical imperfections paraded in shameful print. "I'll send Willoughby over," he said.

"No, I must conciliate them. I know you don't like it, Richard, but I shall handle it discreetly. I'll have a small tea party, invite no one who matters. I must silence her."

"They won't be fobbed off with any little token do of that sort. Don't do anything for the present. Let them simmer a while. The book is spoken of as not coming out for a year. Larry will have his appointment before that without our having to deal with them at all."

"All the worse, to have it come out after he is famous—to have his moment of glory sullied so disgracefully! I won't stand for it, I tell you. I'll ask her here first—to my ball—I ask everyone to that. She won't be noticed in the crowd."

"They are pointed out when they drive down Bond Street and in the Park. Everyone knows them by sight now. They are becoming the talk of the town."

"What is to be done?" Bess wailed in frustration.

"Do nothing. I'll handle it, as I have always managed your problems in the past. Let me think about it. We must have a plan. I'll talk to some people—see how *they* are handling her."

"Very well, I'll wait awhile, but I don't mean to let it hang fire for long. My nerves can't take it."

St. Felix posed a few discreet questions, ostensibly on behalf of a "friend," and learned that the manner of dealing with Mrs. Pealing was to do exactly as she wished. He had never seen Mrs. Pealing; his quarrel was with Miss Ingleside, and he had no intention of letting her win this fall with him. But he soon became aware that she won every match she entered. Not only was she—and of course, that disreputable aunt—lining her purse, but she was beginning to go about to the odd party, as well. The girl was not making her debut, so at least one would not meet her at formal do's. Soon even this shred of relief was snatched from him.

When the list of the young debutantes to be presented to the Queen was printed in the *Gazette*, Miss Ingleside's name was amongst them. The debts had been coming in in such a heady stream that even this was to be afforded. It was not Mrs. Pealing, a *divorcée*, who was to be her official sponsor, but a Mrs. Wintlock. Now who the devil is Mrs. Wintlock, he wondered.

She was not only a friend of the Inglesides from Wiltshire, but a distant connection of Sir James on her husband's side, and she knew them to be a very good family. Her daughter, Stephanie, a good-natured and not overly pretty girl, had attended the same ladies' seminary as Daphne and the two were friends. Having come to London to present her own youngest, she had been delighted to meet Daphne on Bond Street and took for granted she, too, was to make her bows. When she discovered her error, she set up a string of letters to Ingleside Manor that once again threw the house into an uproar.

"What do you think of it, James?" Lady Mary demanded, her own smile displaying clearly what *she* thought of it.

"It's a lot of nonsense and will cost me a bundle."

"It will save sending her back next year," Lady Mary said, thus introducing a whole new concept to the household, for it had never been mentioned that Daphne should make her bows in London. "Once she sees Stephanie Wintlock there, attending all the do's and snapping up a great *parti*, you may be sure she will fix her face to go back to London. And why should she not? Her father could well afford it."

"Her father has better things to do with his blunt. Tiling the east forty, for instance."

"Pooh! What is more important to you, your own flesh and blood or a few acres of mud?"

"The west forty wouldn't be a mud pie if I had it tiled."

"It is money well spent, presenting Daphne."

"Yes, only see where it got your sister—a divorce and a scandal."

"And a count and a millionaire along the way. And Daphne, you know, besides having the looks from *my* side of the family, is as long-headed as you are yourself, James. *She* will not throw away her chances as poor Effie did. You'll see her a countess, too. See if you don't."

"Well, I won't have Effie presenting her," he relented, remembering how she had not bothered to pack her ball gown. He had often thought of that with a sad feeling.

"That would be entirely ineligible. Mrs. Wintlock is a different matter—your cousin's wife. She will do nicely, and it will save our going to London next Season." Always this little reminder was tossed in. Clearly she had fixed on getting Daphne presented, and as the manner mentioned in Cousin Wintlock's letter seemed the easiest way, James capitulated.

Letters were sent back, a bank draft enclosed to cover the additional expenses, and the thing was done. Daphne had first laughed at the idea, but upon consideration she came to appreciate its advantages. A baronet's daughter and the granddaughter of an earl was not suspect, and as no mention of Mrs. Pealing was made in the application, it was accepted.

The apartment on Upper Grosvenor Square was becoming so elegant with all its new blueness that Effie thought she would throw a *soireé* herself, though, of course, the formal presentation ball was to be shared with Miss Wintlock at the Wintlock mansion on Curzon Street.

Aunt Effie bloomed in the sunlight of all her former greatness returned to her. Daphne had observed that the first spate of callers had come once with money and were not seen again, but as the ladies began to go about, to be seen in the Park in a fancy if slightly old-fashioned carriage, to be invited to the odd small party first, then by degrees to better ones, the old friends came back a second and third time, and finally issued invitations themselves. Effie was really rather sweet, they rediscovered, made sweeter to some by the fact that she no longer challenged their marriages and affairs by her former beauty. She looked a quiz, of course, with that blue hair and blue paint smeared on her eyes like an actress, but she was droll and had such amusing stories to tell about the olden days. Not a few found that she was still generous, too, but Miss Ingleside heard nothing of this. Effie knew James's daughter would not approve of her largesse, and she slipped a folded bill into a hand so neatly that the twenty years of non-practice were overcome in a trice. The presence of a very beautiful young debutante on Upper Grosvenor Square did nothing to diminish Effie's popularity, of course. Odd she was staying *there*, but under the aegis of Mrs. Wintlock she was turning up at very respectable do's and being well received.

Aunt Effie did not always accompany Daphne on her excursions, but she was invited to a party at the Leveson-Gowers along with her niece, and this was the most respectable place she had been yet. It would be dignified by the title of a *ton* party by anyone. No less a celebrity than Lady Melbourne was in attendance, sitting quietly in a corner. She was piqued at Lady Hertford's conquest of the Prince Regent, and as she sat looking out on the crowd, she was struck with inspiration. Lady Melbourne was not usually to be found sitting silently in any corner at a party, but on this occasion she had the wonderful company of Beau Brummell to satisfy her, and with a conquest of such magnitude, she didn't bother to speak to anyone else.

"What do you think of the latest rage, Mr. Brummell?" she asked him.

"I doubt she will bring blue hair into style," he

drawled, raising his quizzing glass and examining the new curiosity, Mrs. Pealing, who held court in the centre of a group of elderly beaux.

"She has not your knack for setting a style, but she is quaint."

"England always admires a freak," he returned. "The only country that passes for civilized where cock-fighting and bear-baiting are called amusements and a woman with blue hair is called fashionable. I wonder if green wouldn't be more harmonious with her pink face."

"You don't mean to take her up then?"

"Dear lady, I set the style. I don't follow it," was his languid response. Though a full-grown man, there remained something boyish in his face. A youthful light in the eyes and laughter lurking at the corner of his petulant lips. Life was a joke, and he was one of the few to have discovered it.

"She is a nine days' wonder, I should think. Not really fashionable. Not even you could make her that."

"You forget I brought the Prince Regent into fashion and retained the miracle for a decade and a half. I could make a three-legged sloth the style if I thought there were enough amusement in it to make it worth my while."

"I have had a most amusing notion," Lady Melbourne said.

"Your notions are always amusing, dear lady. Having your children call your husband 'father', for instance." He would only dare to go this far when they were in private, but between the two of them and a good fraction of the rest of Society, it was no secret the lady's offspring had a miscellany of fathers. "What is your latest amusing idea?" he asked.

"Something that might interest *you*, I think. Wouldn't it be fun to see Lady Hertford tremble in her boots?"

Lady Hertford was nothing to Beau, but he was too clever to think Lady Melbourne meant what she said. The reference was to Prinney. Relations between the Prince Regent and his erstwhile bosom bow, Brummell, were recently strained. Its sixteen-year duration was the longest the Prince had ever kept a friend, but even Brummell must become a bore after a while. The little dandy was chomping at the bit to make the Prince appear even more ridiculous than he already was.

He looked across the room at Mrs. Pealing. She had a placid, pink, wide face, a full bosom, and was the undemanding sort of companion the Prince was known to favour. He smiled softly to himself. "Yes, an admirable replacement for Lady Hertford," he said, with a knowing smile. "You're a devil in skirts, Milady."

"Just an idea," she said, a challenge in her smile.

"I like it excessively, but how shall we set about it?"

"You have only to be seen with her in your carriage for him to take a jealous fit and try to oust you."

"My carriage is not reinforced to tote such a load," he replied, letting his eyes travel along the full lines of Mrs. Pealing's blue gown.

"It might be worth your while to have it

strengthened. Really, I would love to see Hertford's face when she hears of Prinney's calling at Upper Grosvenor Square."

"And *I* would love to see Cruikshank's caricature in the shop windows. He would have to use a quart of blue ink for half the picture, at least."

"And a double-width page to get both their corpulent frames squeezed on to it."

"I wonder how the Prince's admiring public would take to his linking up with a thrice-married lady and a divorcée who is blackmailing the half of London," Beau said.

"They'd be bound to think she had a chapter on him in her book and would be sorry to see him paying up instead of letting them read what she had to say."

"I called you a devil, Lady Melbourne, but you are the most ingenious devil that ever was. Wish me well." He arose and ambled forth to attach himself to Mrs. Pealing's train.

Miss Ingleside, watching his progress, could scarcely believe her eyes. Beau Brummell, the leading arbiter of taste in the whole city, was going to speak to Aunt Effie. She couldn't bear to miss it and followed him across the room to hear what he had to say.

"Who is the devastatingly attractive lady in blue?" Beau asked of a bystander, pitching his drawling voice just loud enough that the lady in question might hear it.

Miss Ingleside also heard it, and the sardonic tone in which it was said. Beau, though long the leader of the *ton*, was still a young man in his late thirties, and to think he had succumbed to Aunt

Effie's well-faded charms was not considered for a moment. His reputation as a wit was notorious, and with a sinking sensation at the pit of her stomach, Daphne feared the dandy meant to make a May game of her aunt. And poor Effie no better equipped to deal with him than a mouse with an eagle! She edged closer to hear and, if necessary, to lend assistance.

The introduction was made, and Miss Ingleside listened in dismay as Effie asked laughingly, "So you're the great Beau Brummell? You aren't as fashionable as I imagined. I wouldn't have looked at you twice if I'd met you in the street."

"When a gentleman is looked at *twice* in the street, Ma'am, he is not outfitted as a gentleman ought to be, but is either too stiff, too tight, or too fashionable. And had *we* met on the street, I should not have looked twice at you, either. Having once glimpsed you, my eyes would not have strayed for a moment," he finished with a graceful scraping of the leg.

"You turn a neat compliment. I'll say that for you," Effie allowed.

Ignominy was surely at hand. The great Beau Brummell would not take this piece of condescension without retort.

"Will Madame be kind enough to let me remain awhile with her and see if I can't improve the quality of my compliments to match their inspiration?"

"There's room here on the sofa if you don't mind crowding," she told him, pleased with her new conquest.

The Beau held off a moment at the mention of crowding. His jackets were not to be crushed. He levelled a look at the gentleman on Effie's right, who arose as though he had received a royal command. The Beau hitched up his trouser legs and sat down as gracefully and daintily as a lady.

"Mrs. Pealing, you must tell me all about this book you are writing," he began. "Colburn has been after me to write my memoirs, but I fear after the world has read yours the rest of us must lay aside our pens."

"It will be nothing out of the ordinary, I promise you, Mr. Brummell."

"I cannot credit that *you* have ever had one ordinary thing happen to you in your life," he objected instantly with a gallant smile. "Surely an angel must have led a celestial life, and we shall all be in heaven to read of it."

Daphne thought even her aunt must be suspicious of such heavy complimenting as this, but the elderly lady showed no signs of it. "I've had a few heavenly days in my life," she admitted, "and many that were closer to hell."

"Let us dwell on the sublime," he decreed. "Now to begin with, where is an angel bred? Wiltshire, was it not?"

There was a good deal of nonsense of this sort talked. Effie saw nothing amiss in the Beau's heavy-handed lavishings of praise, and her niece was only confused. A dozen times she felt disaster was imminent, but every time the Beau turned some maladroit remark of her aunt's to an amusing end. Before he left, and he stayed with her a quarter of an hour, he said, "Dare I hope you will allow me the pleasure of calling on you one day soon, Ma'am?"

"I'm sure you're entirely welcome," Effie returned smiling.

"When will it be convenient for me to prostrate myself at your door?"

Daphne, who had joined a few remarks in the conversation, wasn't about to let his extravagance go unchallenged. "A prostrate body blocking the door can never be convenient, Mr. Brummell, but if you care to stand on your feet and sound our knocker, we are at home mornings."

Beau flashed a satirical smile at the young beauty who had been annoying him. "I shall hover a foot above the ground on wings of delight and anticipation till morning, when I shall come to earth and plant both feet on your doorstep. Your obedient, ladies," he bowed, and returned to Lady Melbourne to report success.

"What a plain-looking little fellow he is," Effie said to Daphne. "Mr. Pealing used to talk about him a good deal—said he was the height of elegance, and he with never a bit of a jewel or a thing to him."

"But possibly with the best-cut jacket that was ever invented," Daphne replied, admiring the departing back of the Beau.

"Yes, and a pity there isn't more of him to fill it. Standington now; *there* was a gentleman that made a jacket look like something. But he has very nice manners, this Beau. I daresay it's the manners that have put him over."

Miss Ingleside found his manners the most

objectionable part of him but grudgingly admitted
he had a certain sort of wit.

Mrs. Pealing's signal success was bruited about
town. To have held Brummell's attention for
fifteen minutes set her up higher than ever, and the
news eventually leaked itself back to Charles
Street, where Lady Elizabeth Thyrwite heard it
with mixed feelings. She took the decision that as
the Leveson-Gowers and other quite unexceptionable persons were being blackmailed like herself
into inviting the Pealing to their homes, she would
go along. She sent off a card to an informal
afternoon tea, and if the repercussions were not too
violent, she would also send cards to her ball. That
should buy their silence. The tea for Larry's
flirtation with the lady, and the ball for his loose
lips.

During these days St. Felix spent more time
thinking about Miss Ingleside than his concern for
Larry's welfare warranted. Not for one moment
did he intend to let Bess knuckle under to them, yet
their having crashed the barrier to Society put his
sister in an untenable position. He felt some
compulsion urging him back to Upper Grosvenor
Square and soon found an excuse to give in to it. He
would "feel them out" was the way he justified it to
himself. The silence had been long and resounding
since Bess had briefly acknowledged receipt of her
cheque, and he was curious to know what they
were planning. For some reason unknown to
himself, he did not inform his sister of this second
visit, and, for a reason known very well to herself,
Bess didn't tell Dickie of the card sent to her
afternoon party. Dickie would thunder and scold

and call her a ninnyhammer. Easy for him. *He* was not about to be lampooned in an infamous book for the whole of London to titter over.

St. Felix presented himself again to Upper Grosvenor Square, and once again Mrs. Pealing declared it utterly impossible *she* should meet him. Miss Ingleside, on the other hand, was quite eager to cross swords with him again and point out to him that his dire warnings of ostracism had come to nought.

He noticed during the seven minutes he awaited her arrival in the Blue Saloon that the room had been refurbished and silently calculated how much the ladies had raked in. His first words when Miss Ingleside eventually entered, wearing an ironic smile, were, "I see business prospers, Ma'am." His eyes silently pinpointed the new acquisitions.

"Indeed it does. We have instituted a few renovations to make the place more habitable, and more visitable, for some people have expressed a desire never to return." A pert glance reminded the Duke that he was one of these. "And pleasure prospers as well, despite your fears of our being barred from it." With a wave of her hand she indicated a newly covered chair, where he took a seat and let his eyes wander around the room. No glimmer of approval escaped those eyes, and, in fact, his face was a perfect mask of disapproval.

"I read in the paper you are to attend the Queen's Drawing Room," he said.

"Just so. Not everyone is so nice in her notions as you had feared. And one would have thought that if *anyone* would take exception to a pair of

blackmailers it would be Her Majesty, who is so
strict in all her ideas, but she was very understanding in the matter. We hadn't a single thing to
threaten her with, either. Her charity was entirely
voluntary."

"You haven't made your bows yet, and if the
Queen hears of your doings, you never will."

"I have come to place little reliance on your
lovely threats. Surely no one would be so surly as to
go whispering malicious gossip into Her Majesty's
ears."

"I must confess I am looking forward to the
publishing of this book. Your aunt must have some
racy stories to be flying so high."

"Yes, an interesting compendium of adultery,
gambling, and so on—all the more amusing
pastimes. But at the rate people are coming up to
scratch, I begin to fear the whole will be comprised
of one chapter, entitled Sir Lawrence Thyrwite. A
pity, too, for it promises to be the dullest chapter of
the lot."

"That is why I am come."

"You would like us to enliven it with a little
fiction? I cannot think that would meet with
Auntie's approval. Someone—I forget exactly who
it was—has spoken to us about libel, and we mean
to tell no more than the simple truth."

"Your solicitor, perhaps, was the one who
mentioned it."

"Some disagreeable person of that sort," she
agreed, smiling.

"I am here to discuss Sir Lawrence, not listen to
insults."

"Ah, I was beginning to mistake it for a social

call. I had thought from your delightfully entertaining conversation you were come to take a glass of wine with me, Your Grace." Her lips remained steady, but her eyes were full of mocking laughter.

His blood quickened, and a dangerous flash shot forth from his eyes. "What do you mean to do about it?"

"I am completely reasonable and mean to listen to what you have to suggest. I hear Sir Lawrence is rising in the world—a folio in Liverpool's Cabinet is spoken of. Still, I suppose one's physical appearance is of no importance in that. Liverpool himself looks a good deal like a hippopotamus."

"What I suggest is that you pack your bags and return home before you are found out."

"Found out? The whole town knows what foul deeds we are up to. There is no keeping it secret when the line of victims extends from Upper Grosvenor Square to Whitehall."

"You will not find *me* in the line-up."

"I wonder that I find you in my aunt's saloon, to tell the truth, after your expressing no desire to return. Why is it Sir Lawrence does not come to do his own haggling?"

"He does not wish to."

"Now that is the very sort of behaviour that gives Auntie a disgust of her victims. Top lofty. He wants a good raking down."

"You persist, then, in demanding some payment to withhold the story?"

"If you will but consider, Your Grace, we have never demanded a thing of you or Sir Lawrence. You came of your own free will to berate us and try to push money down our throats. Five hundred wasn't enough—you had to double it, and the insult. We returned the cheque with a very civil note, pretending we were not hurt and that there was some misunderstanding. But these repeated incursions upon our privacy are making us quite short-tempered with the pair of you."

"When you set upon a course of this sort, you must be prepared for some unpleasantness."

"True, but we had not thought the unpleasantness would come from someone we had not approached with our vile scheme. We had not thought people so eager to be blackmailed that they would come barging in twice, demanding the privilege of paying up."

"I am here to tell you we have no intention of paying a sou."

"No one asked you to pay a thing, but your obvious fear of what we might say makes me wonder whether I haven't missed a chapter of the memoirs. I begin to think there is something Auntie is keeping from me. I shall go through the books with a fine-tooth comb and see if I have missed something."

"No, I don't think you miss a trick."

She laughed aloud and said in a warning voice, "Bear it in mind, Your Grace."

"Don't think to threaten *me. My* hands are clean."

"Ah, I see you have washed your hands, but is your conscience clear? No ladybird tucked away in a corner? No wild parties at your Leicester hunting box? No secret vices my avid curiosity might smell out? There is no saying the reminiscences will stop at 1800, as originally intended. I might personally

71

add an epilogue pointing out that the sins of the fathers are visited on the children. I shall suggest it to Colburn."

"Sir Lawrence is not related to me, except by marriage. It would seem more accurate to suggest the sins of the aunt are visited on the niece."

"Auntie will be crushed to hear it is a sin to write a book."

"The sin is in your extorting favours for suppressing your stories."

"It seems it is a chaplain I require, not an attorney. My crimes have been elevated to sins all of a sudden."

"There is no rational discourse to be had with you. I shall leave."

"Without having accomplished a thing! I begin to think you came only to vex me. Take care, or you will find yourself having to return to *this place*."

"Good day, Ma'am."

"*Au revoir*, Your Grace," she waved her fingers. "Till we meet again."

He heard a silver tinkle of laughter follow him as he strode towards the door. He was about to turn around and light into her again but couldn't think of a sensible word to say.

Six

ST. Felix left the apartment in a state of
vexation. He had managed affairs much more
serious than this for his family without a qualm
and wondered that he should let a saucy little chit
bother him so. The worst she could do was to
publish some spiteful nonsense in a year's time,
and Larry's appointment was due any day. It was
in no danger, and the other stories Mrs. Pealing
would be telling were bound to eclipse the romance
with Sir Lawrence. The sense of frustration came
from his not being able to get the upper hand over
her. *He* was the man; *he* the one who ought to be
running the show. She should be trembling in her
boots at his empty threats, as any of his sisters or
any normal woman would; but no, she laughed at
him, and taunted him for returning when he had
indicated he had no desire to do so. The most

galling thing of all was that he knew damned well he would be back for more of her impertinence as soon as he could find an excuse. But he wouldn't let Bess invite her to Charles Street. She would see who was running the show.

While he bolted along in his curricle, the young lady did as she had threatened and went to look over the memoirs, her eyes alert for any mention of Thyrwite. Her most careful perusal brought nothing new to light. Reading the chapters, however, she found some allusion to St. Felix, whose acquaintance with her aunt pre-dated Larry's by some few years; and she reconsidered anew Effie's relationship with the Duke. Effie had become more pliable since her new rise to fame. She was always smiling now, planning new outfits and her little *soirée*. Catching her in a happy frame of mind, Daphne again made a try.

"Aunt Effie, I wish you will tell me the story of your affair with St. Felix," she said in a wheedling voice.

"Lud, Daphne, I've told you a dozen times..."

"Yes, I know you were just friends, but you didn't feel it necessary to hide any other pages from me except those dealing with your 'friend', St. Felix. I know there was more to it than that, and you might as well tell me, for I am imagining the most *lurid* things."

"Is that what St. Felix came about?"

"No," Daphne answered, her interest quickening that he might have done so. How she would love to have something to hold over that sneering face. "I am not standing in line—but you might be

74

yet, Your Grace. I shall quiz him about it next time he does come, if you don't tell me."

"You're making a mountain out of a mole hill. He was just one of my beaux, that's all. When I was married to Standington there were a dozen of them hanging around."

"For shame, and you a married lady."

"Oh, the single ones weren't allowed any fun at all, only the married ladies. But *I* was the only one who paid such a price for her affairs," she said, a little sadly.

"Did you have an affair with St. Felix?"

"No, and not with half the others I was supposed to have had, either. He never suggested an *affair*—he was too much of a gentleman. We spoke of getting married when Arthur sued for divorce."

"That was impossible—St. Felix was already married."

"Oh, yes, and divorce was an even worse scandal in those days than it is today. Practically no one did it then. Bad enough *I* was divorced, but to lead St. Felix to abandon his wife, and he with three children! The present duke was on his way then, as well, and the eldest daughter getting up to the age where she was soon to be presented. I couldn't let him do it. It was too great a sacrifice."

"But he wanted to?" Daphne enquired, feeling a surge of exultant power over her foe.

"My, yes. I lived on at Half Moon Street all through the divorce. Arthur moved into a club. Mrs. Elders stayed there with me for the looks of it. St. Felix came every night for a week to try to talk me into running away with him, but I brought him to see it would not do," she said and then laughed merrily.

"He was quite persistent, I gather?"

"I've never told a living soul this, Daphne, for Georgiana is dead now, and she is the only one I ever told. My, how she laughed, ready to split her sides. She was a love. What I did was this. I took a page from Prinney's book—you remember his trick of pretending to commit suicide because dear Marie Fitzherbert wouldn't have him? I pretended to St. Felix I meant to kill myself after the duel."

"The duel!" Daphne gasped. "I heard nothing of a duel. Oh, but I suppose Arthur had to defend your reputation."

"That wretch! No such a thing. He said he couldn't be duelling with half the gentlemen in London, and he knew perfectly well it was only Ansquith I ever—Well, it was not Arthur who defended my name, but St. Felix."

"Oh!" Daphne was stunned into silence. She had been cheered to hear of the romance between her aunt and the Duke, but a duel having been fought was more than she counted on, or knew quite what to do with. It sounded so very *shady*, and Effie's own husband not being willing to fight made it worse. "How—how did it come about?" she asked weakly.

"Well, the little story about Arthur discovering myself and Ansquith together got about. It happened at Sprocket Hall on a house party. Everyone was talking about it, as people will do. When St. Felix learned Arthur didn't mean to defend my name, he said he would do it himself or other gentlemen would try to take advantage of me. I daresay he thought to shame Arthur into it, but he didn't; and the next thing *I* knew the duel was over and done with, with only a shoulder scratch. They used swords in those days, which is less likely to be fatal than a gun, and much more civilized, I'm sure. Ansquith was touched in the shoulder and St. Felix never hurt at all. He said I *had* to marry him for he was ruined anyway fighting a duel over another man's wife, but we managed to keep it hushed up. Georgiana knew, of course, but she wouldn't tell a soul. So that is when I thought of suicide; oh, not *committing* it, of course, for that would be so very fatal, but of pretending, like Prinney. So the next night when St. Felix came to see me and tried to talk me into running off with him, what did I do but have a glass of wine and vinegar sitting by me. I kept looking at it nervously, and a little later, St. Felix picked it up to take a sip, for I made sure not to offer him a glass. He noticed the odd taste right away, and I knocked it out of his hand as though I were scared to death and said he *must not* drink from that glass. But I let him get one sip first, and he thought immediately what I meant him to think— that I was drinking poisoned wine. He carried on so—oh, my! How it was a sin and worse, and why was I doing such a thing. Well, I gave him to understand it was unhappiness with *his* behaviour that led me to it; that I would sooner *die* than let him ruin his life for me. I told him I loved him too much to see him ruined, and a good deal more nonsense of that sort, with tears and all the rest of it. I told him the only thing that could induce me

not to take my life was for him to go back to his wife
and family and make something useful of his life.
He said it was impossible and even suggested at
one point that we *both* drink poison—so uncomfortable, and awkward, too, me with not a drop of
real poison in the house. I would have looked silly
if he'd pushed it, but I reminded him of his family
obligations at this point, you may be sure. And
made him get rid of his other flirt, too," she added.

"He sounds a sanctimonious gentleman, to be
sure. Had another friend, as well, had he?"

"Well, my dear, everyone had. He was not
considered at all fast or loose. He had a little
actress at one point, for it was never pretended to
be a love match between him and the Duchess. She
took the actress amiss all the same, and they were
not getting along at all when he got after me. The
St. Felixes, you know, were always said to live up
to their full title, the saint and the dukedom, and
the wife's family was full of starch. Her brother
Archie is the Archbishop of Canterbury, if you can
imagine. Ho, and he as full of vinegar as any of
them. But St. Felix went back to being a saint after
I put a scare into him. He and his wife got back
together and there was never any talk about him,
so it was all for the best. How it makes one aware of
one's age. Young Richard a grown man now, and
looking very much like his father, too. Finally
having a son did much to settle George down. He
had given up hope of it and felt that as his brother
Algernon had two sons, the title would be going to
them; and so I suppose that is why he didn't care
too much about running off and making a fool of

himself. Only think if I'd let him and then heard the minute we set foot off the island that he had had a son! Fathers always dote on their sons when they are dead ringers for themselves, as Richard is. Someone pointed him out to me t'other day in the Park. It is why I can't bear to see him when he comes. It brings it all back to me. I believe I loved old St. Felix. Oh, not in the way I love—loved Standington. The first passion is never quite recaptured; but I could have been happy with him if it weren't for Arthur and, of course, the Duchess and his family. But instead of taking up with him, I went abroad and married Mr. Eglinton. I've led a sad and sorrowful life. Such a lot of shame and disgrace I've brought on everyone, but at least I don't have St. Felix on my conscience."

"You are a much-maligned saint yourself, Aunt Effie," Daphne said, very moved by the story. Like everyone else, she had thought her aunt a bit of a mindless fool, but there was a broad streak of kindness, as Mama had always insisted, buried in the foolishness. "Yes, and I wager God has got a special corner of heaven set aside for people like you, too. There won't be many in it, either."

"I hope I am not quite alone," Effie laughed. "It won't be heaven to me if I am not with my friends."

It was a heart-wrenching statement—Effie and her "friends," who robbed her pockets when she was rich and accused her of blackmail when she was poor. And the St. Felixes the worst of the lot— coming with their noses in the air to pay her. She could have ruined the whole family years ago, and they would not be in such eminent positions now.

"So you tore the pages out to hide this story from me, Auntie? You have nothing to be ashamed of in it."

"That was not my purpose in doing it, love. The thing is, Henry Colburn was to see me again the other day and asked to have a look at my memoirs. I wouldn't want him to find out about it. There are some parts of her life a woman wants to keep to herself—or share with only a precious few. You are the only one outside myself who knows the story, and it is not to be repeated. I shan't say a word about Standington in print, either."

"I wouldn't turn the diaries over to Colburn. When did he ask?"

"He has been hinting since his first visit. I ripped the pages out the first night of his visit, but a few days ago I let him scan some of the later books. He wants me to put in things I don't want to. I'm not even sure I'll bother writing the book. We don't seem to have much time for it now since we are going about to parties. Only fancy, Beau Brummell coming to call this afternoon. How I regret Mr. Pealing couldn't be here to meet him. The hours he spent with his valet trying to get his collars starched up, and Beau could tell him exactly how to go about it for sure. It was Beau who started all this starching business. They do say he has his boots polished with champagne, but Mr. Pealing tried it and says it is all a hum."

Effie exulted in her famous caller, and Daphne had a little exulting to do herself. If the Duke of St. Felix chose to come storming in again, she would be hard put not to laugh in his face. But Effie had asked her not to repeat a word and that would be very hard to do.

"Does the St. Felix family not know about the late Duke's involvement with you at all, Auntie?"

"The mother knows. He had given her warning what he meant to do. Such a gudgeon-like thing to do, go telling her. But the others don't, unless *she* told them. I daresay the older girls might have an inkling."

"It was the Duke I was thinking of."

"He wasn't even born at the time."

"Well, if he comes speaking of blackmail again, I might just give him an inkling," Daphne said, to see what her aunt would say.

"Well, maybe just an inkling," Effie said with an arch smile. "But I shouldn't tell him about the duel, dear, for he will feel a perfect fool and we wouldn't want *that*."

"Oh, yes we would."

"That's no way to go about winning a fellow's affection, goose."

"I am not interested in his affection, I promise you."

Brummell paid his promised call, standing on his feet like a gentleman. His carriage, without reinforcement, proved to be up to Mrs. Pealing's and his own combined weight, and with a face betraying to the world nothing but delight in his companion, he drove through Hyde Park, down to Bond Street, then back to the barrier of Hyde Park, to make sure he was seen and recognized. He stopped four times, to make Mrs. Pealing known to

Lords Alvanley and St. Clare, Ladies Blessington and Sefton, and two other groups of untitled notables. Lest this very public gesture should not be sufficient, he also asked permission to accompany the ladies to Lady Melbourne's small rout a few evenings hence.

Daphne still mistrusted his intentions, but no more than her aunt did she wish to pass up the honour of being seen with him. While Mrs. Pealing rode in the Park with Beau, Daphne went with Mrs. Wintlock and Stephanie to a pic-nic at Richmond Park. She was collecting a circle of admirers, and when she went into public with the Wintlocks, the circle was swelled by Miss Wintlock's beaux, as well. Though the girl was not a beauty, she was a considerable heiress and making a small splash.

Daphne was surprised to see that St. Felix made up part of the group. He was older than the other beaux present but clearly not counted amongst the chaperones as being of their number. She tossed him a bold smile, which he ignored completely, turning his back after a mere glance to speak to another lady.

"Do you know St. Felix?" Miss Wintlock asked.

"I have met him. He is very disagreeable," Daphne replied with relish.

"Yes, holds himself very high, but handsome, is he not?"

"I suppose so, if you like that sort," Miss Ingleside returned in a disparaging voice.

Stephanie stared to hear of anyone not liking a tall, handsome duke possessed of wealth and manners.

"He is said to live up to his both titles—sainthood and dukedom," Daphne added, to imply he was too strict for her.

"That'll come as a surprise to his flirts," a Mr. Bosworth said. He was one of Stephanie's admirers.

Miss Wintlock was amazed at the radiant smile this brought to her friend's face. "*Now* she is interested. You see what a minx she is," Stephanie laughed to the group.

"You have my character in shreds at a word," Daphne replied and was immediately at pains to get Mr. Bosworth to herself to discover all details of St. Felix's flirts. What she learned cheered her greatly.

"Very active in the petticoat line," Bosworth informed her with a knowing look. "Well, a bachelor, of course. It's only to be expected."

"Not of a St. Felix bachelor surely," Daphne prodded.

"I don't know about any other St. Felixes, but this one is no dashed saint. Has the prettiest chick in town under his protection. Name is Amy, or Aimée, or some such thing. Well, she ain't French, but you know how those girls give themselves fancy names. A dainty little blond girl. You must have seen her dashing through the Park in that blue rig he gave her, and a pair of cream ponies. She always wears blue, to match her eyes."

"I know another lady who does the same," Daphne returned, smiling more broadly by the minute.

"That so? Well, Amy has brought it into fashion very likely. She's all the crack."

"Yes, I daresay my friend got the idea from St. Felix's flirt," she answered, and fell into an uncontrollable fit of giggles.

She longed to taunt St. Felix with all her new discoveries. To see him standing about looking bored to flinders, as though he had no interest in the young girls, riled her.

He looked towards Miss Ingleside. Indeed several peeps in her direction had taken place already, as she was the only reason he was present. Upon hearing that Mrs. Wintlock and her daughter were to be of the party, he had accepted an invitation to join it. Daphne had been too absorbed to remark his other glances, but she saw this one and nodded her head, smiling broadly. St. Felix took a step towards her, which caused Mr. Bosworth to discover a friend elsewhere. He had told no more than the truth, but there is a disagreeable quality in having to face one's victim so soon after an unnecessary telling of the truth.

"We meet again, Your Grace," she said in a very civil tone, but was at once busy to be teasing him. "Our new sofas and chairs have missed you. I would have thought their being *blue* might please you."

"You seem well amused today," he said with a cool look. Not a trace of a smile himself, though he was very much aware of the attractiveness of the impish smile facing him. He was wondering just what that reference to blue meant, and fearing he knew.

"I am never so well entertained as when I am discovering new scandals," she replied enigmatically.

"This seems an unlikely spot for it, with innocent green nature everywhere."

"It is people who cause scandal, not places."

"I see nothing scandalous going forth."

"You would see the exalted Duke of St. Felix speaking to that disreputable Miss Ingleside if you had a mirror. Even in Richmond Park I am bent on mischief."

"And find it, unaccountably, a matter to boast of."

"We will all boast a little of our successes, even in our less worthy schemes."

"Was it your aim, then, to engage me in conversation, as you speak of success?"

"Indeed, no, this is a quite unlooked for honour. I had hoped for no more than a glance from afar."

"You knew I was coming?" he asked with interest.

"No, how should I? Even the pleasure of a glance was not anticipated in advance, thus robbing me of half the pleasure. It is the looking forward to a thing that gives a good deal of the enjoyment. I might have been *aux anges* all last evening had I known you were to be here. But I have something quite different to anticipate now."

"Am I to assume that cryptic utterance relates to myself?" he asked, regarding her suspiciously.

"That assumption would be less wrong than some others you have made."

"What are you up to now?" he asked baldly.

"What is the likes of me ever up to? Chicanery, and if you are at all curious you must bring a bale of gold to Upper Grosvenor Square and find out."

A glint of amusement appeared briefly in his

cold grey eyes. "You are aware of my aversion to that place. Can't you tell me here?"

"Give up my secrets without receiving a fortune in return? How can you take me for such a flat!"

"I take you for a brass-faced gypsy, Miss Ingleside."

"Unlike *some* people, I do not try to pass for what I am not, *Saint* Felix."

"We do not emphasize the saint."

"Indeed we do not. *Au contraire*, Your Grace." She left with a taunting smile to return to her own group, where Miss Wintlock called her the slyest thing in nature, to be flirting with St. Felix after letting on she didn't care for him in the least.

Daphne returned to the apartment to be regaled with the story of the fine drive Effie had with Mr. Brummell, so very droll and amusing, and really he would be quite a fine gentleman if only he would dress up a little more smartly.

"He is considered the apex of good taste in matters of fashion!" Daphne objected.

"Yes, but he hasn't a jewel or a trinket about him, poor soul. He is not too deep in the pocket, I daresay. But he moves in the very best circles for all that. He is to take us to a party at Lady Melbourne's."

This was thrilling enough, but there was a more interesting piece of news still awaiting them. The mail, unopened in Effie's usual careless fashion, was eventually gotten around to, and there in the clutter of bills and the odd card of invitation was a note from Lady Elizabeth Thyrwite requesting the pleasure of their company at a tea party to be held in two days, the afternoon of the evening they were to go to Melbourne's rout.

"I don't believe it," Daphne declared.

"Oh, dear, I shouldn't think we will accept this one," Effie said, pushing it aside. "You know I do not like to have anything to do with *them*, because of their dear papa. I think it would be bad *ton*, dear, for me to be in their company. Quite a few people know of that business, though it was so many years ago."

"You're right. We shall decline," Daphne agreed for reasons of her own that had nothing to do with the *late* Duke of St. Felix. What a joke to snap her fingers under his nose and show him what she thought of this great treat he had been threatening to withhold. And what on earth had gotten into him to let his sister send the card?

"You send off a nice note saying we will be unable to attend," Effie suggested. "It includes your name, too, so it will be all right for you to answer for us both."

"I'll write it, you sign as you did the other one. You are my hostess, and I won't have him think *I* am running the show."

"Larry would never notice a detail like that. I doubt he will see the letter at all. It comes from his wife."

"Still, you sign it," Daphne insisted, not choosing to disabuse her aunt of the idea that it was the loose-lipped Larry whose opinion interested her.

"What a gay visit it is turning out to be after all," Daphne said as they sat over a cup of cocoa after returning from a successful outing at the opera.

"We're taking in everything except Almack's," Effie agreed happily. "And it is not at all interesting, my dear. You would not like it in the least. A very dull sort of a do they put on. All the very best people, and there is no hope of getting you a voucher when you live with me. I wonder if you ought not to move in with the Wintlocks. They have asked you a dozen times, I'm sure."

"If it is so dull, I shan't mind missing it," Daphne replied, a little confused at the mixed reference to the place just made.

"No, it would not be at all agreeable. I wonder whether Mr. Brummell might not get *you* a ticket, if it were made perfectly clear to him that *I* am not interested in going myself."

"I don't want to go without you."

"There is no way in the world *I* would ever get in, dear child. A divorcée. I might as well expect to be invited to tea with Queen Charlotte, who thinks divorcée another word for she-devil."

"I don't mind missing it. Miss Wintlock is not going either. Indeed, a great many girls who go everywhere else aren't being invited there."

"No, only the *very best* people are let in. Why, they turned the Duke of Wellington from the door last year only because he didn't wear satin breeches or some such thing. Still, it is a pity. You would be invited if it weren't for me. If your mama had brought you, you might have gotten in."

"I don't mean to worry over missing one dull party. We are having a marvelous time. I never thought it would be half, or a quarter, so much fun.

Why, do you realize I brought my paint box with me thinking to pass the time taking your likeness?"

"I had a feeling. Didn't I tell you I had a feeling, and my feelings are never wrong."

"Indeed you did tell me. Do you have any other feelings?"

"Yes, I have a feeling we are banging our heads against a stone wall in thinking to get you into Almack's. Though now I come to think of it, Daphne, Lady Melbourne's daughter, the Countess Cowper, is a patroness, and she will be at her mama's rout for a certainty. Perhaps when she seeks us with Mr. Brummell..."

"Still harping on that? I am not interested in Almack's. Let us have done with it. Think—no, *feel* something else."

A tremor shook Effie's stout frame, and she turned quite pale.

"Auntie, what on earth is the matter? Are you having an attack?" Daphne demanded, positively worried at her aunt's condition.

"Arthur!" Effie said in a weak voice.

"Arthur?" It was necessary for her niece to run over a few gentlemen before recalling that Arthur was Lord Standington, the first husband.

"Standington," Effie explained, putting a hand to her head to steady herself.

"What about him?"

"I had a feeling. One of my *feelings*, Daphne. I sensed he was—I don't know. Not present, exactly, but—somewhere about. Thinking of me. I wonder if he has heard about this book I am supposed to be writing, though I haven't put a word on paper for two weeks. He is in Ireland. He can't have heard. Unless someone wrote him a letter. Do you think anyone would be low-lifed enough to do that?"

"Maybe he takes the *Observer*," Daphne suggested. A few minor "feelings" of Effie's had come to pass—the appearance on their scene of an old friend forgotten for twenty years had been anticipated a day before her appearance, as well as the stepping up of their social life. Daphne was coming to entertain some respect for her aunt's power.

"To be sure, he always did read it. He would have seen Colburn's notice. Daphne, do you think he thinks I am going to write about *him*?"

"He must know you better than that."

"No, he doesn't know me at all. He thought I loved Ansquith, only because I let him ... Oh dear, I'm sure James would have a fit if he knew what I am saying to you. But he was very lonely, my dear, and his wife did not understand him at all, he said. Only I come to think that when a man says *that*, she understands him only too well. But I didn't *love* him, despite what Arthur thought. It was nothing more than a flirtation. Well, perhaps a *little* more, but only once. But as to its being an *affair*, it was no such a thing."

"Arthur is thinking of you. That's what it is. Some people have that power. It seems to run in our family, for Mama has these feelings, too. She knew when my father overturned his carriage and broke his arm. We were just sitting down to dinner one evening when Mama dropped the gravy boat and turned pale, just as you did, and said 'James.' It is very odd. She knew something was the matter with him and had the servants sent out. They found his carriage overturned and himself with a broken wing. She had her feeling at the very time he overturned, she calculated later."

"Well, the feeling is gone now," Effie said with relief. "But it was there. He was thinking of me, I know it. Dear, I wonder if I should write him and assure him the book is in no way to touch on our affairs? Do you think I should?"

"Yes, he must be worried in case you should announce to the world how he refused to fight to protect your honour!" This churlishness on Standington's part bothered Daphne very much, the more as it was St. Felix who had risen to her defence. And perhaps most of all because Effie herself took no account of it.

"I never *did* tell anyone but Georgiana and you, and he must know I'm not likely to start telling *now* what I have kept mum for so long."

"It is not my place to advise you, but as you have asked, I see no harm in writing to him. It is clear you still care for him, and it will be an excuse to be in touch with him again. There is no saying what might come of it."

"All that would come of it is a scolding letter. He is a good deal like James, now I come to think of it. How very odd that Mary and I should both choose such hard, uncompromising husbands. And our father was the very same. We knew what a dance he led Mama and should have been smarter. You'd think that would have been a lesson to us."

"Do what you think best," Daphne replied and was struck with a strange feeling of her own. St. Felix, too, was one of those hard, uncompromising gentlemen, like Papa.

Seven

ST. Felix had not been around to see his sister for a few days, and as he wished to find an excuse to allow him to return to Upper Grosvenor Square without admitting to himself that seeing Miss Ingleside had anything to do with it, he dropped in on Bess.

It happened that she was eager for Dickie's opinion on quite a different matter from the Pealing affair, so for the first ten minutes they discussed whether gold or green should be the new decor for Larry's office. It would require doing up as he was on the verge of becoming a minister in Liverpool's Cabinet. There was no saying what great statesmen might be dropping in to pass the time of day with him. Larry wanted red, but his wife knew better than to let his opinion influence her. In matters of taste, she was guided by no one, while listening to Richard as having occasionally a sane suggestion. St. Felix found it a little odd that Bess should not even mention the matter that had been uppermost in her mind for so long, and had at last to bring it up himself.

"You haven't heard anything from the Pealing woman?" he asked.

"No." Deciding to take the plunge, she went on to add casually, "She hasn't answered my invitation yet."

It wasn't to be slipped in this quietly. "What invitation?" he demanded, bristling.

"Oh, didn't I tell you? I decided that as everyone is inviting them now, I would send them a card to a little tea party I'm having."

"Bess, you gudgeon!"

"Well, the Leveson-Gowers had them to a rout, and Lady Melbourne is having them to her do. She was driving in the Park with Beau Brummell, and the girl, it seems, is even being presented. I decided to ask them, but they haven't answered."

"They're not coming!" he declared with a very firm resolution, although it was not his own home. "Remember your position, Bess. Your uncle an Archbishop and you inviting a divorcée to tea. Someone must maintain a sense of decency. They must not come."

"They might," she warned.

"Not one toe do they set in this door."

"Be reasonable, Richard. I have already invited them."

"I'll uninvite them."

"You will do no such a thing. Besides, they haven't accepted."

"They'll be here with bells on. I can't believe you are so green as to give in to a shameless blackmailer."

"Everyone else is inviting them."

"*We* are not everyone else."

"Maybe *you're* not, but *I* am," she insisted, then frowned as she tried to figure out what she had just said.

"If you ladies had all banded together and showed them cold shoulders, this would not have happened. What is to become of Society if any trollop with a smutty story may make her way into the very best homes with a threat of revealing her past? Her sort should be whipped at the cart's tail."

Bess shrugged. "It is done. They go everywhere, and the girl is not so bad, they say."

"She's worse than the old lady! The boldest hussy that ever was!"

"There is no need for you to have anything to do with them. It is only a small tea party. I hadn't thought to ask you." But of course Dickie must be invited to her ball, where the Pealings' presence was to be explained by the largeness of the do.

"You needn't worry that I mean to have anything further to do with them," he said angrily, already in his mind standing in the Blue Saloon. "You might at least have spared me the embarrassment of going there vowing we'd never give in an inch, if this was what you intended all along."

"I never told you to say that! I begged you to take them the money, and when you refused to do that, you said you'd think about it. Well I don't know what you *thought*, but you certainly didn't *do* anything, and I was left to handle it all by myself."

"I went back to see them."

"What did they say?"

"More sauce from the young chit. Nothing to the point."

"It seems to me it is the aunt you ought to be dealing with. What has the niece to do with anything? I'm sure your intentions are of the best, Richard, but they have outmanoeuvred us. The first time *you* have ever failed in any undertaking. I made sure you could handle one stupid little old lady, but as she has bested you, we must now pin on a smile and pretend we are very well satisfied, like everyone else."

"I'll be a pickled herring if I do," he said and arose to stomp from the room. St. Felix did not take kindly to defeat, and to defeat at the hands of an upstart young chit from the country, he positively revolted.

Miss Ingleside herself was so delightfully busy at this interval that she scarcely found an hour a day to wonder when she would see St. Felix again. There was her presentation at the Queen's Drawing Room and all its attendant preparations to be dealt with. Not only her presentation gown, but several others as well had to be fitted and trimmed. Their having to be made up in such a hurry landed more than one at her door unhemmed, to be taken up by her own flying fingers. Various outings with the Wintlocks occurred, and there was her aunt's *soirée* still being planned and prepared, growing by leaps and bounds till they both wondered how the small apartment was to hold the more than fifty people already invited. There were letters to be written home telling Mama and Papa about her grand time, and there was as well the occasional visit from Mr. Colburn, who was becoming impatient with their slow progress. Not a page had he received from them.

One event of much greater significance than all the others combined came to pass, and Effie had not the merest trace of a feeling connected with it to give them warning. Word had been drifting to the Prince Regent's ears of a new Incognita on the London scene. In his set, the Incognita at Upper Grosvenor Square was not Miss Ingleside but her aunt. He had not personally clapped an eye on the delectable Mrs. Pealing since those ancient times when she had been a countess. He had some tender memories of her in her green youth, a dark-haired elf of a girl with blue eyes and the promise of a fullness of figure to come e'er long. He thought she must have ripened to a more appetizing armful by now, filled out a little, as he had done himself. The memory alone might not have impelled His Highness to have his team hitched up and himself laced into his creaking Cumberland corsets, but when it was reported to him that Beau was squiring the woman around town, he had a card sent to her—really, he must get her moved to a better address—and was soon following his card.

Daphne was in alt to think of such a visitor— The First Gentleman of Europe—but Effie made little of it. "He used to be always with us on Half Moon Street—but when I was right on the corner of Piccadilly with Arthur, not after I moved across and a block north. I don't believe he ever came to me after I was demoted to Mrs. Eglinton. Arthur was quite jealous of him. He was always jealous of the wrong ones."

"What is he like?" Daphne asked eagerly.

"He used to be all airs and graces, but Beau hasn't a good word to say for him. Strange, too, for I thought they were inseparable. Something must have come up to cause a rift."

This remark would have revealed to anyone who had any small connection with Society just how far and how long Mrs. Pealing had been out of it. The rift had occurred over a year ago and was fast gathering to a head. The Beau, from his preeminent perch by the Prince Regent's side, had taken to insulting all the great ones, but when he remarked casually about the Prince himself, "I made him what he is, and I can very well unmake him," he went too far. He was on the brink of being unmade himself but was still hanging on to his laurels.

"What should I wear?" Daphne asked next.

"Just an afternoon gown, dear. Prinney wouldn't want you to outshine him. He will be sporting some sort of a uniform, I make no doubt."

Miss Ingleside wore her best afternoon gown, a new rose-sprigged muslin with a wide sash at the waist and a rose-coloured ribbon in her hair. She felt terribly underdressed when His Highness arrived wearing a chestful of medals and ribbons, quite hiding his dark blue jacket. On his nether parts he wore a pair of yellow trousers and looked rather like an overgrown pear with a coat on. He came with the intention of casting off Lady Hertford, but with some slight misgivings as to the ravages of thirty years on Mrs. Pealing's beauty, he brought along his present mistress for protective colouration, in case he did not wish to keep up any acquaintance with the new flirt.

He hadn't been there long before he decided to switch. Effie was as delightful as ever. Teeth still in good repair, and with a set of dimples (actually creases in her plump cheeks) when she smiled that he had forgotten. Comparing the two aging ladies as they sat side by side comparing each other, he had to give the palm to Mrs. Pealing. Besides the charm of novelty, her memories and conversation—all of matters thirty years old— recalled to him his golden youth. Campaigning for Fox, the parties at Carlton House, the building of his Pavilion at Brighton and the early revels there. She was as good as a tonic, and he was in need of a strong one the way the press and Parliament were treating him lately. He left a new man, about to take on a new woman, and as he descended the stairs, he met St. Felix on his way up.

The Prince nodded, St. Felix bowed formally and said, "Your Highness," and each wondered what the deuce the other was doing there. "The old biddy," the Duke thought, while the Prince surmised, "It'd be the young filly he's after," and Lady Hertford had more than an inkling what was going on in both minds.

Mrs. Pealing dashed to her room to write up the Prince's visit in her diary, and Miss Ingleside sat smiling in satisfaction. Not knowing the relationship in which Lady Hertford stood to the Prince, nor what he had in mind with regard to her aunt, she was very happy, indeed, to see Effie achieve such a pinnacle. Daphne was positively glowing and looking very beautiful, indeed, in her new gown when St. Felix was announced, to top this splendid day. She didn't immediately grasp the import of his opening volley.

"What have you got against that pair?" was his first remark but saved from ill manners by the smile that accompanied it.

"What? Oh—you cannot think we are holding *him* to ransom!"

"I wouldn't put it past you," he replied, taking up a seat without waiting to be offered one.

"No, no, we draw the line at *royal* dukes. You smaller fish are fair game, but Prince George and his brothers are above our touch."

"What was he doing here?" he asked. From having so often had Miss Ingleside on his mind, he felt he knew her better than he actually did and didn't realize the question was an impertinence till it was spoken.

"I don't know. There is more than one gentleman whose reason for coming to our apartment is not quite clear to me. Yourself, for example."

"But I was invited the other day at Richmond Park, if you recall."

"Invited to bring us gold! I don't see any."

"And you never will, Miss Ingleside. Not from me, in any case."

"You are come for another argument then," she sighed wearily, while her eyes sparkled with happiness. "What are you going to tell me you won't do this time?"

Again he smiled, with something coming quite close to naturalness. "Not argue with you, as that is obviously what you have in mind to make me do."

"I think you just wanted the pleasure of admiring our new blue room again."

He ignored this repetition of his predilection for blue and said, "How did you enjoy your presentation at the Queen's Drawing Room?"

"It was a dead loss. There wasn't a bit of scandal to keep me busy. I might as well have stayed away for all I gained there."

"No, you are not going to lure me into an argument, Miss Ingleside. I know that even *you* did not go *there* looking for scandal."

"You are determined to wave a white flag at me then?"

"Oh, no, a white flag signifies surrender, does it not?"

"And is it only to be a truce?"

"Hostilities may reopen any moment. When I hear your intentions regarding my sister's tea party, for instance," he said leadingly. Yet he was becoming resigned to the idea she would attend and even taking some pleasure from it. With the Prince Regent calling on Mrs. Pealing, it was foolish to go on calling her an upstart. She was brazen and she had a regrettable history, but she had originally been of a good family and had apparently managed to reinstate herself within the bounds of Society.

"So you know about that! I rather thought Lady Elizabeth had squirmed out from under your thumb and sent the card without your permission."

"The card did not have my approval, as you

rightly imagined."

"I am happy to hear your sister treats your commands with the disrespect they deserve."

"What makes you suppose I issued any commands in the matter?"

"That disagreeable Friday face you are wearing. And don't tell me you didn't come here to argue. You mean to demand that we not accept the invitation. Well, I shall take the wind out of your sail and inform you we have sent a refusal."

"Indeed! May I know why?"

"You *may*, if Lady Elizabeth decides to tell you. I cannot feel it necessary to make an explanation to anyone, but her."

He thought he had come to tell her she must under no circumstances accept the invitation and suddenly found himself growing angry that she had refused it of her own accord. Mrs. Pealing scarcely figured in his reckonings at all. It had become an affair between himself and Miss Ingleside, and she had outdone him again. "But is it not what you wanted?" he asked, confused.

"Certainly not! We never wanted anything of the sort. My aunt feels that because of the peculiar circumstances between herself and you—your family—it would not be quite proper for her to attend." She observed him closely, to try to gauge whether he understood this reference to his father.

He did not seem to. "The 'peculiar circumstance' between Sir Lawrence and Mrs. Pealing does not appear to bother my sister."

"No, it does not bother my aunt either, for there was very little to it after all. I speak of a circumstance much closer to home—to yourself, that is."

"If you mean to imply there was something between your aunt and myself, I might just point out to you what I should have thought would be clear..."

"To the meanest capacity!" she threw in.

He blinked. "The disparity between our ages. She is old enough to be my mother." He thought they were joking and even let another smile come within ame's ace of lightening his countenance.

"And might almost have *been* your mother, during her affair with the *late* Duke of St. Felix."

The smile died aborning, and St. Felix's brow darkened. He was silent for thirty seconds, catching his breath and digesting the infamy of her charge. "That is a lie!" he said in frigid accents. "My father was *always* a man of the highest principles. There has never been a whisper of any scandal connected with him. He lived the life of a saint."

"Saint Bacchus, perhaps!" she answered, her resentment at Effie's ill usage coming to the boil.

"If you put one word of such a calumny into that scandal-mongering obscenity you and your witch of an aunt are writing, I'll drag you through every court in the land on a charge of libel!"

"What a delightful prospect for you, Your Grace! A totally new mud lustre added to the family escutcheon. I daresay it would add thousands to the sale of the book."

"You are *utterly* without scruples. I thought blackmailing those who are guilty was the worst of it, but I see now there is a lower rung to your ladder of which I was unaware. You mean to smear the innocent as well with outright lies, after they are in their graves and unable to defend themselves. Well, I take leave to tell you, I will not stand still for this, Miss."

"I don't expect you to. I'll see you dance to my tune before many days are out."

He stared at her as though she were a devil incarnate and didn't doubt for one moment she would do exactly as she threatened. Even in the midst of his anger, he knew he must protect the family name. "What is it you want from me?" he demanded.

"A voucher to Almack's," she replied with a sweet, innocent smile, this having been mentioned as the one unattainable object.

"Impossible! They have rules at Almack's. It is restricted to ladies and gentlemen of quality."

"My father's ancestors were amongst the first baronets created by James I."

"Impressive!" he said with a withering glance. "My ancestors were amongst the first *dukes* created by William the Conqueror five hundred years previously."

"And on my mother's side, we are related..."

"On your *mother's* side you are, unfortunately, related to Mrs. *Pealing*. You might as well expect a voucher to heaven as to Almack's."

"I haven't given up hope of either one. And I'll let you in on a little secret, Your Ancient Grace, *I* do not hold the two to be comparable as *you* seem to do. Heaven stands a little higher in my priorities."

"It is an odd way you go about securing your priorities."

"So it is, but efficient nevertheless."

"What bargain have you struck with the Almighty to wedge your way into the Celestial City?"

"I have undertaken to lessen the pride of certain noble gentlemen who hold themselves very high. Pride, you must know, was an abhorred thing according to the Bible, to say nothing of going before a fall."

"You have the quotation, like everything else, inaccurate, Ma'am. Let me refer you to a more pertinent one. 'A liar should be once heard, and thrice beaten!'"

"I agree with you, Sir, and wonder that you lie to me. Ask your elderly friends and relatives whether your St. Papa-Duke was not in love with my aunt, whether he did not sit on her doorstep night after night, begging her to run off and marry him. Yes, my 'unfortunate' maternal relation might almost have been your mother. She was tempted to accept his persuasions, being divorced herself, but she could not care for the little actress he kept on the side. Neither did your mother, according to the memoirs." She knowingly tampered with the truth to make him angrier and realized that the inkling she had given him of the truth had not been given in any form Aunt Effie would approve of; but it was really intolerable that he should speak so of Effie after she had saved his family from ruin.

"We hear a good deal about these apocryphal memoirs. I make no doubt the two of you sit up nights inventing them and scribbling them in blood."

"No, no. Vitriol! *Blue* vitriol. Auntie dislikes red, and her blood is not the right shade of blue."

"I had not observed her to have much sense of discernment in her shadings of blue," he answered with a contemptuous glance at the many tints of it present in the room.

"Not so fine an eye for shading as your ladybird, perhaps, but I think Amy stole the idea from Auntie all the same." She didn't think it could be possible for him to look any angrier than he already did, but it was. He had jumped to his feet several insults ago and now took a step towards her chair. She thought he meant to strike her and was delighted rather than frightened. Even Papa had never been in such a towering rage as this.

She continued with her attack. "When I am writing up my epilogue on the present generation, Society might be interested to hear what St. Bacchus Junior is up to between visits to the House of Parliament and the Archbishop's Palace. Tell me, Your Grace, for I like to get all the little details correct, does your mistress favour the French spelling of Aimée for her name, or does she acknowledge her English background and call herself plain Amy?"

He stood stock still, his face red with the stress of controlling his hands from going around her neck. "I don't want to see your face or form at my sister's party," he said.

"Then you had better stay away from it, for I have changed my mind—a lady's prerogative you know, along with a little gossiping—and have decided to attend."

"I *will* stay away, and so will the rest of London."

"How disappointed your sister will be, after writing up all those cards and having a batch of food prepared. You are not very considerate of her. I have often suspected as much. Mr. Brummell will be disappointed, too. He has been *begging* me to go with him and has assured me it is the only place to be tomorrow afternoon."

"You are a good pair! An upstart clerk's son and a..."

"A baronet's daughter. But the title only dates from James I, of course. Give us another five hundred years and we may achieve *your* degree of arrogance. Ah, you are leaving, Your Grace," she said in surprise as he turned on his heel. "And I didn't think to offer you a glass of wine. How remiss of me. I had the hemlock all prepared as a special treat for you, too." The door slammed, and she was not sure he had appreciated her parting shot.

Left alone, Miss Ingleside sat down with a pensive face. Now should she go to Lady Elizabeth's tea party or not? Having refused made it difficult, and having pretended she would have Mr. Brummell's escort made it almost impossible to go, as she wished to, without him.

But Fate, so kind to us in our less noble schemes, gave her a hand out of the latter difficulty. Having learned from the tattle-mongers that he had induced his fat enemy to call at Upper Grosvenor

Square, Brummell must make sure the Prince continued his calls by a few more outings with Mrs. Pealing himself. He came the next morning with a bouquet of blue roses. That was impossible, but by purchasing white ones and leaving them stand in a solution of ink and water overnight, he had got a little of the liquid to go up into the petals and give them a blue veining.

"Oh, Daphne, only look at this!" Effie gurgled, excessively pleased at the tribute. "Blue roses. It is a miracle. However did you think of it, Mr. Brummell?"

"More to the point, how did you *do* it, Mr. Brummell?" Daphne asked, intrigued.

"Roses are sweet, obliging things," he answered with one of his sardonic smiles that promised a compliment so elaborate as to amount to an insult. "When I whispered into the petals' ears that Mrs. Pealing's favourite colour was blue, they grew so sad at their white tint that they turned blue in grief."

"You are absurd," Daphne laughed, amused in spite of herself.

"My absurdities are the making of me, Ma'am," he agreed solemnly.

"I have wondered what has made you the King of London. It wouldn't do to suggest your tailor had anything to do with it."

"Oh, no, I made Weston, and quite a few others, respectable. Even that fellow, ah, Prinney, was accepted in Society for a few years while I extended my patronage to him."

"Absurd and dangerous," Miss Ingleside warned him.

"In the land of the blind, the one-eyed man is king. When I came to the city, it was struggling blindly for something. I surveyed the scene and could only deduce from the symptoms that absurdity was its goal. Having a certain knack for it, I raised it to an art form, and have been crowned King of the Land of Fools. But you and your aunt run me a close second," he added.

Effie looked offended, but the quick-witted Beau had been bored with this stuffed cushion since he had met her and sensed a mind more to his liking in the niece. "We entered the race quite inadvertently," Daphne replied, understanding precisely what he was getting at and gaining a little more respect for the dandy by his assessment of himself and the world of London Society.

"I believe you did, but, having entered it, you seem in some danger of beating me at my own game and I think we ought to join forces."

"Why not? London requires a Queen of Fools as well as a King."

"And as the Prince has two princesses, I shall have two queens," Beau smiled.

"We shall share the honour at the Queen's Drawing Room, Auntie," Daphne said.

"Queen Charlotte runs the Drawing Room," Effie pointed out, sitting perplexed in a corner. When Daphne became James's daughter, she was incomprehensible.

"We are only funning," Daphne consoled her.

Mrs. Pealing found no fun or sense in the discussion, and the Beau turned his charm on her, soon guiding her out the door to his carriage. But after tooling her through a few well-crowded streets, he returned to have a word with Miss Ingleside and to enquire whether she would do him the honour of accepting his escort to a showing of paintings at Somerset House that same afternoon.

She was delighted and added offhandedly, "And perhaps you will escort me to a tea party afterwards. Lady Elizabeth Thyrwite has invited us..." She looked to Mrs. Pealing to see how the idea went down. She read stark horror.

"Not me!" Effie said loudly.

"I will be very happy to. I promised Lady Elizabeth to drop in," the Beau said graciously and left, well pleased with his morning's work.

His original aim had been to bring about a liaison between the Prince and Mrs. Pealing, but it would add a fine feather to his cap to show the world that while Prinney favoured the dull, stupid old lady, *he* had walked off under his nose with the young Beauty. They would be in each other's company, he and the Prince, and he was honing up a few sharp aphorisms to stun the world.

When he had left the apartment, Mrs. Pealing asked, "What made you change your mind?"

"St. Felix particularly mentioned the tea party yesterday, Auntie, and I dislike to disappoint him when he is quite sure I, at least, shall attend."

Effie took on the posture of receiving a feeling, but in somewhat diminished form. "What is it?" Daphne enquired. "Do you sense disaster? Pray tell me if you do and I shan't go to the tea."

"No, it was more an idea than a feeling. I was just thinking, wouldn't it be fine if you could land St. Felix?"

Daphne turned a pretty shade of pink and

declared there was nothing less likely in the whole world.

"Don't say so, my child. His father was quite a fool over me, I assure you, and everyone who knew me in the old days says we are much alike. And what glimpses I have had of young St. Felix tell me he is not so very unlike his papa. It is a very good notion, and I think you should go to the tea party and be friendly to him if he is there."

"Well, I don't think *he* means to be there."

"Why did he want you to go then? He will be there, depend on it. The whole clan stick as close together as peas in a pod. It is St. Felix's doings that Larry is to be made a minister, you know. The head of the family always runs the show in that tribe."

"Yes, I think he tries to in any case. Well, if he is there, you may be sure I shall say 'how do you do' to him."

Eight

AFTER his fight with Miss Ingelside, St. Felix posted directly back to his sister's house to enquire of her if she had ever heard anything of an affair between their father and Mrs. Pealing.

"Of course not. The idea's ridiculous!" she declared. "Who is saying such a thing?"

"Pealing's niece. She claims father asked the woman to marry him."

"What nonsense!"

"I knew it could not be true. Father was always so—well, almost holy. He never looked at another woman for as long as I knew him."

"Yes, he straightened out remarkably," was the frightening response to this.

"What do you mean? He *never* ran around—there was never any talk of that sort attached to him. I don't know of any gentleman of whom more good was spoken than Papa, unless it were Uncle Archie, the Archbishop."

"Ages ago—oh, years and years ago, Dickie, when you were hardly born—he had a few affairs; nothing to signify. And your Uncle Archie, too, for that matter. But it was opera dancers with him, as a rule. Papa's girl was an actress, I think, and some other woman. But I was very young myself and only remember listening to Mama and Papa fighting behind closed doors."

"An actress?" he asked. She didn't care for the little actress he kept on the side, he thought to himself.

"Yes, a redhead, I think she was, from the Theatre Royal; but it was the other one Mama was really concerned about. It was not Mrs. Pealing, for Mama called her Lady something or other. They even mentioned divorce. I remember lying in bed trembling lest it should happen. How selfish children are. I was due to make my bows in a year or two, and all I thought was that I would be disgraced, and never gave a thought to what poor Mama must be going through. And Papa, too, for that matter. I don't suppose he relished the idea of divorce; and he must have been dreadfully in love to have even thought of it, for in general all he ever spoke of was keeping the family together, and everyone doing his part, and so on."

"You don't know who the woman was? Mrs. Pealing was once a Countess. Mama could have meant her."

"It couldn't have been Mrs. Pealing."

"Why not?"

"Because they haven't mentioned it to you, and they'd be demanding a couple of thousand pounds if they had such a story as that in their book."

"Or a voucher to Almack's," he added, chagrined.

Elizabeth ignored this aside. "I don't know what I am to do about that pair. They have sent in a refusal to my tea. They are clearly holding out for a larger party. And now with Prinney calling on them I daren't refuse. I shall have to send tickets to my ball."

She thought she would hear an argument against this plan, but Richard was sunk in some deep reverie from which there was no rousing him, and he hadn't heard.

"Uncle Algernon!" he said, out of the blue.

"Yes, I asked him, but with his gout, you know, I don't look to see him. He usually hobbles to my balls, but he won't bestir himself for a tea party."

Her brother arose and walked from the room in a brown study. Before many minutes he was sitting at his uncle's bedside. Algernon Percival was his father's younger brother by two years and presumably well aware of all the amorous history of the late Duke. Algie had always been a grouchy old fellow and no favourite of any of the nieces or nephews. He complained for a while of his negligent treatment at the hands of his family; then, giving the cap on his head a poke that sent it sliding at a rakish angle over one eye, he said, "And why are you come, eh? Run into debt, I suppose, and with I don't know how many thousands a year coming to you. Don't expect me to bail you out. I have two sons of my own to provide for. Not that I ever see hide or hair of them."

"I'm not here for money, and never have been, Uncle. That shot was unworthy of you. I want you to tell me something."

"There's a change, then, for *you* to let anybody tell you anything. What is it?"

"Who is the woman father was running around with thirty years ago?"

"Mrs. Robinson," the uncle answered unhesitatingly.

"You can't mean Perdita?" Richard asked, incredulous. The shock of the revelation was great enough to knock Mrs. Pealing temporarily from his mind. Though it had happened so many years ago, it was still spoken of as a legend, the Prince of Wale's first public affair with the pretty actress, Mrs. Robinson, who appeared at the Theatre Royal as Perdita in *A Winter's Tale* and soon appeared in public with her Florizel, Prinney.

"She was over being Perdita when Arthur took up with her. She received pretty short shrift from that commoner of a Prince, if you want the truth of it."

"I'm not sure I can take any more truth. You mean to say *my father* took that notorious whore for a mistress? The whole town must have been buzzing with it."

"I don't care for your language, St. Felix. There was nothing wrong with Mrs. Robinson. The town was talking, all right, but it didn't last long. Your father found someone he liked better. He wasn't always the cardboard character he was after you were born. I guess having a son to keep an eye on him smartened him up."

"Oh, that is what I am really come about," Richard said, recalled to his business. "I knew about the actress, though I didn't know it was Perdita. My God... But who was the other one?" His fists were clenched in dreadful anticipation of what he would hear.

"I don't know," his uncle said.

"You've *got* to know!" Richard shouted in frustration. "Think! Try to remember."

"Keep a civil tongue in your head or I'll have you shown out. I ain't senile. I haven't forgotten. I never knew. He kept it close as an oyster, to protect the woman's name. Though from what I remember, she didn't have much name to protect. Reputation, I mean. He was afraid of making bad worse was what he actually said. Something to that effect." He gave the cap another clout that sent it off his head entirely.

"A divorcée, by any chance?" Richard asked.

"It wasn't Richmond's wife, if that's what you mean. She was run well to seed by then. I wondered at the time if it wasn't Lady Standington. You wouldn't know her, but she was..."

"I know her. What makes you think it was she?" he asked through clenched jaws.

"Everyone in town was trailing after her, and that old fool of an earl so busy raiding everyone else's nest he didn't see what was going on in his own. I knew her a little myself, and I know George used to call on her; but he might have done it to throw me off the scent. He knew I was trying to find out what he was up to, and wouldn't I have keel-hauled him if I'd managed to discover it. Something gave me the idéa it was Lady Standington." He sat frowning, trying to recall.

"Who would know for sure?" Richard asked.

"Nobody except your mother. If *I* didn't find out, you may be sure no one else did. And I *trust* you are not proposing to pester her with your questions. Oh, it was no secret he was one of her court, but I don't know how far it went."

"I have to know."

"Why? Why the devil do you want to go raking up that scandal? George settled down and behaved himself for close to thirty years. Seems to me you could show a little respect for your father's memory. Your maternal uncle an Archbishop— another reformed character."

"I am depraved on both sides," Richard said, sunk in gloom.

"Ho, *depraved!* Archie has become holier than the Pope, I'll have you know, and never did have any bit of fluff worth a second look either. *He'd* have been glad enough to take up with Lady Standington."

"Oh, my God! How did she find time to juggle so many lovers."

"She was quite good at it!" Algernon laid his head back on the pillows and laughed in happy memory. "What a girl she was. But not too bright. I often thought if she'd had half as many brains as she had looks she could have nabbed one of the royal dukes, and for a husband, not a lover. All she lacked was a tupporth of brains, poor girl. But they never have both, worse luck."

"She has, worse luck," Richard said, but in such

a low tone that it escaped his uncle's failing ears.

"How does Larry's promotion go on? Any word of that?" Algernon asked.

"Nothing definite has been announced. Wouldn't anyone know about father's lover except Mama?"

"Yes, the lady herself, whoever she is."

"I can hardly go about asking every lady over fifty if she had the honour to be my father's mistress."

"What difference does it make who she was? He had one, and that's what you wanted to know, ain't it?"

"No, I must know who she was."

"If you ever find out, give her my compliments, for she was a real lady."

"Then she can't have been Mrs. Pealing."

"Lady Standington was the name I mentioned."

"Now Pealing. She has remarried twice and been widowed. Why do you say she was a *real* lady?"

"Lord, boy, she could have had your father for the snapping of her fingers. He was mad for her; and where would you be now if she had, eh? He told me himself he meant to divorce Agnes and leave the country with his lover. Felt he had to tell me that much, for I was to be in charge of looking after everything while he was gone; but he never told me her name, just in case she wouldn't go through with it. Well, maybe he didn't mean to divorce your mother—but leave her anyway, which is possibly even worse. But whoever the woman was, she had the sense and breeding and charity to turn him down. And did it in such a way that she made him ashamed of himself. He went back home and straightened out. *You* had something to do with it. Your being a son pleased him no end, and I daresay he took pains to give *you* no notion of his scarlet past. He was always afraid you might have developed his streak of foolishness."

"It can't be that damned Pealing creature!"

"I see no reason for you to traduce Lady Standington's name. She was a very nice girl. If that fool of a Standington had stood by her and run Ansquith through instead of dragging his wife through the divorce court.:.*He* was a fine one to take exception to her having a *cicisbeo*. He was after everything that wiggled, so long as it wore a skirt. An awful man he was. Jealous as a green cow, and proud, too. I just remembered something that might help you."

"What?"

"That lady George was after—she liked blue."

"Oh, God! Why did you have to go and remember that."

"He had a ring he was trying to give her. I don't believe she ever accepted it. Well, I know she didn't, for I saw it sitting on Bess's finger on her next birthday; but it was a sapphire, and he said in a fit of poetry that it matched the lady's eyes, and it would match her gowns, for she wore a deal of blue. Lady Standington wore a lot of blue. Now *that's* what it was made me think it was her. *That's* what it was," he repeated, triumphant at this feat of memory.

St. Felix arose, feeling an old man. His father— that cardboard saint he had been revering all these years—was just flesh and blood like the rest. But mixed with his anger and disappointment was a little pity. Poor father, to have met Daphne after he was married and saddled with a nurseryful of children. Countess Standington, he corrected himself! But everyone said they resembled each other in Mrs. Pealing's youth. He could not say, never having yet met Mrs. Pealing.

"Thank you, Uncle. I think I've discovered what I came to. I hope the gout isn't too painful."

"Bah, pain. I care nothing for that. It's this damned lying around in bed that kills me. It's what you've got to look forward to, my boy. Runs in the family. Got your father and it'll get you."

This reminder of mortality naturally did nothing to lighten St. Felix's spirits. "Do you come to Bess's party?"

"Not her tea party. I don't much care to hear geese cackling, but you can tell her I'll be at her ball, if I ain't dead. She might drop around to see her old uncle once in a while. It wouldn't kill her."

"I'll tell her."

He left, to consider how to silence the blackmailers, for in spite of the recent shaking of his world, he did not wish to see the family name trailed through the mud. He was now rather eager to meet Mrs. Pealing. He had glimpsed her in her carriage but had no idea of her face. He frowned, imagining Daphne Ingleside's face grown old and fat. He began to feel it might not be impossible to procure a voucher to Almack's for the young lady, as the Prince Regent and Beau Brummell were both on visiting terms with her. In any case, he felt that it was imperative to see her; and for this reason he came down off his high horse and went to his sister's tea party the next afternoon.

He went early and immediately asked his sister, "Has Miss Ingleside not got here yet?" His quick view of the six persons present had already told him the answer.

"She isn't coming. I told you I had a note turning it down."

"She's coming."

"Have you been to see her again, Dickie? I thought we agreed that you would have nothing more to do with her."

"Complications. It is now imperative that I have a great deal to do with her. I'll speak to you later, and if any of the patronesses from Almack's are to be present, butter them up well. We have a favour to request."

"Lady Sefton is coming. I asked Lady Melbourne, but she is throwing a do herself tonight and is sending her daughter, Countess Cowper, in her place."

"Good. I'll give Emily a go. She is always susceptible to flattery."

"Especially from handsome gentlemen."

They parted, and for the next three-quarters of an hour, St. Felix's eyes only left the entrance way to scan the crowd for patronesses from Almack's. He was polite to Lady Sefton and fawning towards Countess Cowper, who took very well to his buttering up.

Bess went to him once and said, "I don't believe she can be coming. And Brummell stayed away, too. He told me he would be here, the beast."

There was a little ripple of excitement, and several heads turned to the door. Beau Brummell sauntered in, a picture of sartorial elegance, though he wore the simplest outfit possible, with no .jewelry except a plain gold ring. His well-cut coats and carefully tied cravats were the envy of every aspirant to fashion. He dressed with care and style, and once he was dressed he forgot his clothing and turned his mind to being entertaining.

"Thank God, he is come," Bess said, breathing easier. "Who is the *ravishing* creature with him?"

"Miss Ingleside," her brother replied.

"Dickie, you never told me she was an Incomparable! If that is how the Pealing looked in her youth, I shouldn't blame Papa if he *did* succumb to her."

She sailed forth to make the King and Queen of Absurdity welcome and to introduce the young lady to any of those present who had not already the pleasure of her acquaintance. With Beau Brummell at her side making the conversation sparkle, Miss Ingleside appeared to great advantage to Countess Cowper; and when Lady Sefton had her alone a minute to discover she was the daughter of Sir James Ingleside of the Wiltshire Inglesides and the granddaughter of Lord Basford, Earl of Basford, the portals of Almack's were in a good way to opening for her. There was the Pealing to be overcome, but a well-to-do Mrs. Wintlock of whom no harm was known proved to be an acceptable chaperone. That Miss Wintlock, too, must be provided a voucher was no problem; the girl was on the verge of receiving an offer from Lord Henry Viddington, young son of a good family.

"You know nothing to the young lady's discredit, Emily?" Lady Sefton enquired of Countess Cowper.

"No, no, quite unexceptionable. Mama has asked her to a rout this evening. Of course, it must be made clear her aunt is not to come with her. A little touchy that, but Mrs. Pealing understands these things. She has been around long enough and, if she is in doubt, Beau will straighten her out."

"I'll give her a voucher before she leaves, then. My, such a crowd around her. I'll have to wait."

"I notice St. Felix is interested. He has hardly taken his eyes off her."

"And *you* off him. Take care, Emily. Yes, the girl is a charmer. One cannot but wonder that she chose to make her bows from Mrs. Pealing's home," Lady Sefton remarked.

"It is the Wintlocks who are actually presenting her. Odd she doesn't stay with them."

"But then La Pealing's company would be more entertaining. Prinney was to call, you know. I bet Lady Hertford is in the boughs."

"Oh, she went with him," Emily said. The affair was being closely followed in the Melbourne circle. "But I doubt she will the next time."

Miss Ingleside made a most favourable impression, and despite his most assiduous observation, St. Felix could not get near her without an unseemly jostling, which he did not care to undergo. He waited his chance for a private word, which did not come till she was on her way out the door, with Beau Brummell at her side. While Bess said goodbye to Beau, Daphne turned to the Duke with a pert smile.

"Did you forget to tell everyone, including yourself, to stay away?" she asked.

"I must speak to you."

"You are speaking to me."

"Alone."

"You have discovered from your flirt how she wishes her name spelled? Just tell me whether it is to be the English or French version. We don't require solitude for that."

"About my father's past."

"I doubt you can tell me much I don't know about that."

"I don't want the story printed. What is the price for your silence?"

"We have already discussed it. It is a voucher to Almack's. And, really, I begin to think you are getting off too lightly, for Lady Sefton was not at all put out at the newness of my family. She called me 'dear' twice and said I reminded her of Miss Gunning, which is a compliment, I was given to understand. She married two dukes."

"I'll see what I can do. It will be very difficult—they are strict. Perhaps Countess Cowper might be persuaded."

"I can certainly not accuse you of not *trying* to persuade her. If my name were Amy, I think I should not have cared for your attentions to her this afternoon." In fact, even as Daphne she was not entirely pleased with his behaviour.

"She is a married woman! If you are intimating I was carrying on a flirtation..."

"Much that would bother you St. Felixes! In your heart of hearts, I think you demand some sort of ineligibility from your women. Married ladies, divorcées, actresses."

"Blackmailers?" he asked with a sneering smile.

"I didn't mean that!" she said angrily.

As they talked, it was Lady Sefton and not Countess Cowper who approached them with the cherished voucher in her hand. "A ticket to our little party Thursday evening, Miss Ingleside. I hope your chaperone—you will see it is Mrs. Wintlock's name on the card—will bring you. And her daughter, of course. It is for the three of you."

"How very kind of you, Ma'am," Miss Ingleside said, accepting the ticket with a smile. With a flourish of her fingers, she waved them under St. Felix's nose. "It seems we must reconsider the price of silence. Like candles and green peas and everything else, it is going up. What was impossible has turned out to be so extraordinarily simple, I begin to wonder whether I shouldn't ask for the moon."

His talk with Lady Elizabeth terminated, Beau turned to offer Miss Ingleside his arm. St. Felix bit back some angry rejoinder and said, "I'll call on you tomorrow, Miss Ingleside, with your permission."

"Miss Ingleside has promised me her afternoon," Beau said, patting her hand in a proprietary manner that inflamed his grace.

"In the morning, Miss Ingleside?" Richard asked.

"Yes, you may bring that—thing to me in the morning. On a platter of course!" she reminded him.

Beau looked surprised. "Is it a cake you speak of?" he asked.

"No, Mr. Brummell, a pie. *Humble* pie," Daphne smiled.

Richard glared at her with murder in his eyes. "I'll be there," he said.

"The pleasure will be all yours," Daphne answered, and with a wave of her little gloved hand that still held the voucher, she was off.

It was a long while before the last visitor had left the tea party and the brother and sister could get down to serious discussion. "She wasn't so bad," Lady Elizabeth began. "What I can't understand is why the girl ever lowered herself to become involved in this underhanded business of the aunt's, for she might have been accepted without such a trick. Very charming, and she has got the Beau right under her thumb. He *never* was serious about any girl, Dickie, in all the years he has been on the town."

"No mother with a pittance of mind would let him dangle after her daughter. He is amusing, of course, and has a certain *ton*; but his breeding is not what anyone of good blood would care to take into the family, and he has no fortune to speak of."

"Still, there are wealthy widows and rich old spinsters aplenty who would have snapped him up fast enough had he ever looked twice at them. He has been unsusceptible till now, and I think it the biggest item of the Season that he is caught at last."

"Caught? Caught by a blackmailer who is bearleading him into buying her silence by this show of gallantry!"

"Pooh! Everyone knows Beau is a clerk's son with no money to speak of. He can't be paying her not to tell what everyone knows already. It is not that."

"I don't know what she may have on him; he may be doing it for a lark. He threatened last year to bring the mad old King into fashion, and may have decided on Miss Ingleside, instead; but that is nothing to us."

"Brother, you are as blind as a bat. Beau is in love. Miss Ingleside is the very lively, intelligent young girl for him. They are as well suited as wine and cheese."

"She's not that big a fool; but, in any case, it is nothing to us. I have been to see Uncle Algernon."

"I should go, too. How horrid, having to visit him only because he is laid up with gout. We never bother with him when he is well, nor he with us. I don't see that I should have to drag over to Belgrave Square only because he soaks up wine like a sponge and makes himself sick with it."

"It is not the opprobrium of sick visits I refer to. He told me about Papa and the mysterious woman."

"Really! Who was she?"

"Mrs. Pealing."

"It can't be true! How can we keep them quiet? Dear Mama—to have to go through that again. And Larry—this will reflect on him!"

"It will reflect on the whole family, and we must put a muzzle on them."

"Yes, certainly. How much? We'll have to get our sisters to join, Dickie. They'll want thousands, and I don't see why you and I must bear the whole burden. Betty's husband is rich as a nabob, and Alice's expenses are very small, living in the country year round. We'll all go shares. Did they give you any indication of how much they are asking?"

"She mentioned the moon."

Bess rolled her eyes in despair, and then sent Richard home while she jotted a note off to her two sisters, requesting them to curtail their expenses, for they must each come up with a thousand pounds to save the family's name.

Nine

⦿⟞⟝⦿

The rout at Lady Melbourne's turned out to be one of the more interesting occasions of the Season. In one of the long saloons there was the Prince of Wales holding court, presided over by two princesses, but not his two wives. Lady Hertford sat on his right hand, wearing the mask of tragedy, and Mrs. Pealing on his left, wearing no mask at all but her usual smiling face. It was to the princess on his left that most of His Highness's remarks were addressed, and it was her glass that was kept full of wine. The Prince was a famous jilt. His casting aside of Perdita in his youth had been the forerunner of the long list of similar rude castings-off. His first wife, Mrs. Fitzherbert, had lasted longer than most of his women, certainly much longer than his formal wife. Princess Caroline had been really only a ship passing in the night, leaving in her wake the necessary heir. But both his wives had been replaced long since by a series of plump matrons, and it was obvious to the world that Lady Hertford's turn had come. Her repudiation was more public and shameful than some, but, on the other hand, no worse than plenty of others. Titters erupted behind fans and raised fingers, and bets were beginning to be taken on which duo would emerge from the trio, with odds running long in the newcomer's favour.

When one tired of laughing at the Prince, one could always nip into the next saloon to hear Beau Brummell exchange quips with his new protégée.

"You will forgive my not offering to rise and procure you a glass of wine, Miss Ingleside, but I have a touch of gout in my leg, and it is my favourite leg, too."

"I wouldn't dream of disturbing you, Mr. Brummell, for I know very well you require all your time to think up clever things to say to make us all look like fools. But not quite such a fool as you look yourself. That must be my little consolation."

"Watch your manners, young lady. I have had better people than you put out of Society for less impertinence."

"You have had so many put out that there is a rumour the rejects are setting up their own club and calling it the Ten Thousand."

"No, they are calling it the Court," he returned in a drawling voice.

"You will find yourself ruling over an empty roost if you keep up with that sort of comment," she warned.

"No roost can be said to be empty when *I* am ruling it."

"Very true. It would be full of hot wind, and good for that gouty knee your old age has brought you."

"Do they not teach good manners in Wiltshire, Miss Ingleside?"

"Indeed they do, and unlike London, they also practice them in Wiltshire. I was quite at a loss how to go on when first I came to London; but I was advised to take yourself as a model and have made such advances that I am nearly a perfect savage now."

"Observe myself and practice a little more, and if you are a fast learner, you may yet achieve some small degree of perfection. I find you to be tolerably conversable," he said, struggling to keep pace with her sharp tongue but on the whole satisfied to have a chance to show off.

"And not yet so *intolerably* conceited as my instructor, I hope."

"Conceit has no part in the bearing of a lady or gentleman."

"I am happy to see you don't preach what you practice, Mr. Brummell."

A little crowd hovered around to examine the curious sight of a young lady who gave back to the great Brummell blow for blow.

When it was time for refreshments, Mr. Brummell waited till he saw the Prince Regent, in an unusual fit of gallantry, approach the table; then he arose and offered Miss Ingleside his arm to confront the Prince.

"Some lobster patties, Miss Ingleside?" Beau offered, and she accepted.

"None for me. I am on a diet," he added in a loud voice. "I do not intend to go to fat in my old age as some unfortunate gentlemen do. There is nothing so vulgar as a stomach. No tailoring can conceal it. In the very worst cases, a fellow may even sink to wearing a corset to brace himself." He just barely glanced at the Prince's creaking bulk as he spoke.

Miss Ingleside, aware of the feud between the two, wanted no part of it. She scowled at Brummell, for the Prince, though pretending not to hear, was becoming red about the ears.

"Does your aunt care for lobster, Miss Ingleside?" the Prince enquired, ignoring completely Mr. Brummell while making clear the food was not for himself.

"Yes, very much, Your Majesty," Daphne answered in a humble voice.

"That aunt of yours has questionable taste," Beau said loudly. He looked at the lobster, but the sting in the tail of the speech was felt by the Regent, and he longed to retaliate.

"I wonder if anyone thought to fill a plate for Lady Hertford," Beau went on. "I see her escort has only one and it, I believe, is for Mrs. Eglinton— er, Pealing."

The Prince could take no more. He set down the plate and returned to his seat, to let footboys serve him and his party as was his usual custom.

Lady Melbourne took Mr. Brummell severely to task, and he felt himself that he had gone far enough for one night. Miss Ingleside was vexed at having been used by Beau. The Prince did not care to exchange public jibes with the rapier-tongued fellow, but he felt he knew the cause of the anger and smiled to himself to think he had captured the charming Mrs. Pealing out from under his arch rival's nose. He was determined to attach her after that evening, and went alone the next morning to call on her. He had not foreseen that Miss Ingleside would be present ("have to get rid of the girl") but at least she didn't have Brummell at her feet, as was only too possible. She soon had a caller of her own in the person of St. Felix.

For a short five minutes the four mismated persons sat trying to think of innocuous subjects of conversations, then St. Felix turned aside to Miss Ingleside. "I came to talk about that book with you, Ma'am. Shall we go to the library and have a look at it?"

While he sat in the saloon, his eyes had been trained on Mrs. Pealing. That this squat, pudgy female had ensnared his father was almost impossible for him to believe, and that she had ever borne the slightest resemblance to Miss Ingleside completely impossible. He couldn't see a feature in common.

Miss Ingleside went with him. There was no library in the apartment, but she was grateful to get out of the Prince's presence. He was markedly cool to her after last night's rout. They went to the little study where the memoirs were kept and occasionally worked upon.

"I seem to be tripping over a prince every time I come here," St. Felix said.

"I don't hear the Prince complaining," she replied, taking the seat behind the desk and indicating the only other chair for her caller.

"You will hear it if you persist in making him look a fool, with Brummell's contrivance."

"What busy little bee has been running to you with stories of last night's party?"

"My sister was there. She said you were the centre of attention, and behaving perfectly outrageously."

"What would you expect of a parvenue whose family can only be traced with credit for two hundred years?"

"A *modicum* of behaviour, when it is her aim to pass herself off with credit in Society."

"Now here is a new twist," Daphne said, smiling ironically. Yet she was far from happy with her own performance. "Are you setting out to reform me, Your Grace?"

"I am not so quixotic. I am merely warning you. God knows why I should bother. It would serve you well to be cast out of Society, as you should be, but I must confess to a grudging admiration for your brass. One does tend to side with the hero of a picaresque story."

"So now I am a knave and a rogue, am I?"

"You always were, but when you clash horns with the Prince Regent, you take on a good deal more than you can handle. You may have won a battle last night, but you will lose the war. Brummell is on his way out. It is only a matter of time, and a very little time, till he is finished."

"Everyone defers to him."

"He's in debt to his neck—gambling—and he lives on a very small income. If you are wise, you will switch sides while there is still time."

"Why do you bother to tell me this? You have wanted to see me beaten since the first day you came to this place."

She found him to be without an answer. He didn't know himself. He despised mushrooms, but somehow Miss Ingleside had become more than an upstart trouble-maker. He would fight to the death to prevent her revealing anything to cast aspersions on his family. His whole aim was to best her, but he would dislike to see her disgraced and humiliated, as she would be if she got the Prince turned against her."

"Is this what you are offering me in lieu of a moon?" she asked. "The benefit of your advice in payment for our silence regarding your father? You must know I have found your reading of Society's whims somewhat inaccurate in the past. You have a definite tendency to overrate any misdeeds on *my* part."

"You are in need of an adviser, my girl. It was foolish of your family to send you here alone."

"Yet I have managed to make myself acceptable to everyone, except yourself. I have obtained a voucher to Almack's, and as you find a prince cluttering the apartment every day, I don't think I need fear reprisals from him."

"He comes to see your aunt. He was not friendly towards yourself. In fact, if he proceeds in his customary fashion, he will set her up in a love nest where you will definitely be *de trop*. And it is the best thing that could happen to you, too. You would do better to reside with the Wintlocks."

"Love nest! You are insane. She wouldn't dream of such a thing. It isn't that sort of a relationship, though. I might have known *you* would think so."

"It is running to long odds at the clubs today."

"You can't be serious! He has only called twice, and all they do is talk of the old days."

"He ain't exactly a red hot lover, Miss Ingleside.

His passionate days are over, but he likes a plump bosom to rest his head on."

"Oh, what a mind you have!"

"And what a greenhead you are, to have been turned loose in this wicked city without a protector. I don't know what your family was thinking of."

"I have my aunt's protection."

"Negligible. She permits you to entertain gentlemen callers alone, and that is not done. She sits and smiles while you make a show of yourself in public."

"*You* are the only gentleman I have ever entertained alone!"

"But could you have chosen a worse one?"

"No, I couldn't; but you needn't try to tell me she would set up house with that—that *Prince*—for she wouldn't. She laughs at him behind his back."

"But not to his face, I think. She wanted to make a comeback, and she has apparently succeeded; but it won't do you any good if he takes you in dislike, and he will most certainly do so if you carry on with Brummell. They have been at daggers drawn this year."

"And I suppose you think *I* am on the verge of being set up in a love nest with *him*!"

"No, he can't afford it."

"How fortunate for me. Otherwise, of course, I would hop at the chance and find myself amongst the muslin company, with the Amys of the world."

"Highly unbecoming talk in a young lady. Who told you about Amy?"

"One may hear it on any street corner, Your Grace. It was, I believe, the corner of Haymarket and Piccadilly where it first came to my ears."

"It will make dull reading in your epilogue then. As well known as a ballad. But I think it was at Richmond Park that you discovered it. I noticed a particularly enraptured smile alight on your face when you were talking to Mr. Bosworth. I have Bosworth to thank for this favour."

"Why should you care if I know?"

"I don't," he answered very promptly, and felt a pronounced desire to run Mr. Bosworth through with cold steel. "But I really came to discuss with you the business of my father. I know all about it now."

"You know very little about it!" she said sharply, and would have told him more but for Effie's injunction.

"I know at least that we are indebted to your aunt. I should like to hear any more you have to tell me in the matter."

"*I* can tell you no more. It is my aunt's story, and her book, not mine."

"You are co-authoring it, I believe?"

"Just adding a few semi-colons to give it a literary touch. You overestimate my involvement in the work."

"I have been led to. You will never let me speak to your aunt. I was beginning to believe she had died and you were availing yourself of her memoirs illicitly."

"You were not beginning to believe anything of the sort! You are only trying to annoy me. She did not wish to see you. She finds you disconcertingly like your father."

Joan Smith

"How can she, when we met only briefly?"

"She has seen you. There is a physical resemblance, I believe."

"But that should be to my advantage, at least so far as she is concerned."

"It doesn't appear to be, but as she is caught out in the open today, it is an excellent time to approach her."

"We have nothing to do but wait then. Tell me, Miss Ingleside, why is it you reside with your aunt when it is the Wintlocks who are sponsoring you?"

"I had no notion of being presented when I came to London. It was only supposed to be a family visit."

"And why were you *not* being presented in the regular way?"

"What a lot of questions! Papa does not hold with London goings-on. Only see how they have made a fallen woman of Aunt Effie! He feels Mama is a good deal better off, and she was married without having a Season."

"Then he should not have let you come at all. To come and not be presented was worse than anything."

"More blackmail," she smiled. "Mama said that if he didn't let me come when Auntie invited me, she would have Effie to live with us."

"It runs in the family, I see. How pleasant."

"All families have their little vices. With some it is insanity, with others lechery, and others blackmail. There is a little bad in the best of us."

"Yours appears to be tainted with a touch of the viper's tongue, as well as blackmail. I understand your meaning very well."

"And here I thought you were dull-witted. There—he is leaving!" she said, upon hearing the noise of closing doors; and together she and St. Felix went to the Blue Saloon, to catch Aunt Effie already on her way to slip past them to her chamber.

"The Duke of St. Felix would like a few words with you, Auntie," Daphne said, and received from her aunt a glare that said "traitoress." She received another when she abandoned her relative with the Duke and went to her own room. St. Felix, too, was put out at this treatment but was interested enough in Mrs. Pealing to find himself well occupied. He still could find no justification for his father's affair with her.

"I have been trying to see you these several weeks," St. Felix began, and stopped before saying another word. The little woman was smiling bemusedly on him, her blue eyes actually glazing over with an unshed tear. He felt suddenly foolish, and very ill at ease.

"How very like St. Felix you are," she said, and shook away the tears.

"You were well acquainted with him, I am given to understand."

"We were friends, but so many years ago—a lifetime ago."

"That is what I wish to speak to you about."

She shook her head. "I suppose my niece put you up to this. I have told her and I tell *you*: what is past is past, and I have no intention of dredging all that up again. Some things are best left buried."

"And best left unpublished as well, Mrs. Pealing."

141

She looked at him in shock. "There was never any question of publishing any reference to that, Your Grace."

"You didn't intend to include it in your memoirs then? I was given to understand otherwise."

"May I ask by whom?"

"By your niece."

"The minx! She has been making a May game of you; depend on it. Very likely she has taken you in aversion, for she never can tolerate you overbearing gentlemen. She knew perfectly well I would not mention my husband and I would not mention St. Felix. Indeed, I don't know what kind of book it is everyone thinks I mean to write. I have told them all a dozen times it is a book of reminiscences, mostly relating to unusual happenings abroad—a sort of travel book of conditions in Europe a quarter of a century ago. How anyone should think I meant to write ill of them for the whole world to read is beyond me. And especially when it would involve myself as well," she finished up a little less philanthropically.

"That is not the understanding of the world at large."

"It is the understanding of anyone who bothered to ask me; and while you are here, you might reassure your brother-in-law, Sir Lawrence, that his name will nowhere appear in the book, either."

Having gained his major point, St. Felix was about to raise this minor one himself. "I understood from your niece..." he began, then stopped to consider his words. The niece, though she had occasionally contradicted herself, had certainly indicated more than once that she was not blackmailing anyone.

"You must have riled her," was Effie's reply. "Well, you did, for she mentioned it to me. I'll tell you what it is. It's guilt and fear that brought the world to my door. That and a misreading of my character. Yes, you may stare—the image of your father—the fact is I wouldn't consider for a minute doing what *they* would apparently do if they were in my shoes. It would never have occurred to me to wash anyone's dirty linen in public. I was shocked when I tumbled to it what everyone thought. I never would have if Daphne hadn't dropped me the hint. The evil is all in their own minds, and a very poor idea it gives me of them."

"When it was announced that Colburn was to be your publisher..."

"He would like a more scandalous book than he'll get, I grant you; but I told him what I mean to do, and I'll stick to my guns. Or maybe I won't bother to write him a book at all. It was to fill the time, but the time seems to be filling itself more agreeably than scribbling would do. In any case, if you're here to ask me not to write anything about your papa, your trip was unnecessary. It's an insult, and if St. Felix were alive, he wouldn't have let you make such a cake of yourself," she finished.

St. Felix was, of course, delighted to have his fears squashed. Once he became accustomed to the idea that there was nothing to fear from the lady, he began, like others, to be curious about her, even to like her plain speaking. She rattled him off, just like his mama. "I imagine you could tell some interesting stories if you wanted to."

"I could tell you stories—especially *you*—that would stand your hair on end, but I shan't."

"You know, I suppose, of my father's affair with Perdita?"

"Ho, that baggage! I don't know what the gentlemen saw in her. A lantern jaw, a face a mile long, and little pig eyes. But it was the Prince's affair with her that set her up in her own conceit. St. Felix didn't care for her in the least and was happy enough to be rid of her once... But I said I shan't tell, and I shan't."

"I can be a perfect pattern card of discretion, Ma'am, and I own I am curious."

"The whole world is curious. Colburn is right in thinking there would be a market for my stories. No one wants to be written of themselves, but how eager they are to read of others!"

"He was my father," St. Felix explained his rampant curiosity and thought he might discover the whole if he kept her talking long enough.

"All the more reason for me to be mum. You've nothing to be ashamed of in him. No worse than you are yourself, I daresay."

St. Felix shot her a quizzing smile, looking very like his late papa, though he didn't know it. "Your niece has been painting you a picture of me? A pity she hasn't your discretion."

"She didn't say a word. What are you up to, eh? An actress or an opera dancer, I'll warrant. At least you ain't a married man to be making advances to girls. Lord, how St. Felix could have wanted me to run... But never mind that. You'll not get anything out of me."

"Two can play at this game of silence. You tell me why you wouldn't run away with Papa, and I'll tell you all about my harem."

"How could I run away with him, and your poor mama about to bring you into the world? Wouldn't it have looked fine, a married man fighting duels..." St. Felix came to rigid attention and said not a word. "Not that anyone knew about it."

"It was kind of you to hush up that business about the duel," he said calmly.

"Who told you about that? It must have been my niece, for she is the only one in the world who knows—I daresay a few suspected."

"Oh, my Uncle Algernon knows the whole thing," St. Felix said.

"He don't know about the suicide, for I had an oath of St. Felix not to tell."

St. Felix felt his insides shrink and searched his memory for a relative who had died mysteriously.

"That put a good scare into him," she laughed.

"It must have given him a turn all right," he said, wondering how to discover the identity of "him."

"Of course I would never have been such a gudgeon as actually to *do* it."

"You'd think he'd have known better than to believe it," St. Felix agreed, surmising that he at least knew now the victim *manquée*.

"Well, the fact of the matter is, your papa wasn't thinking very straight; but, there, we won't mention a word of that. How's your mama?"

"Well," he replied, and wondered if he had the whole story yet. "But Papa behaved pretty well once you put a scare into him by pretending you were going to commit suicide," he said leadingly.

"I don't take all the credit. Having a son helped. Yes, your papa grew up at last, which is more than can be said for the Prince, poor fellow. As foolish as ever."

"Still dangling after all the pretty ones," he roasted.

"If he thinks to make *me* his next love o' life he has another thought coming, and so I told him to his face. That is just what I don't need—to be set up in style for two or three months till he tires of me and then held up to ridicule and scorn."

"You turned him down, then?"

"Indeed, I did; and there's no need for you to be mentioning it either."

"You forget we are two deaf mutes, you and I." He doubted the lady's discretion, however. With the best intentions in the world, her secrets were there for the taking. She might not plan to publish her stories in printed form, but if she were to continue going into Society, there wasn't a chance in hell of them remaining secret. His aim achieved, he arose. "I owe you an apology, Ma'am, and am happy to make it. May I have the pleasure of calling on you again?"

Effie's blue eyes narrowed. She didn't think it was to see herself that St. Felix wished to return to her apartment. "We'd be happy to see you. Any time," she added grandly.

"I'm not so sure 'we' will be happy, but having *your* permission, I shall come."

"Now the ice is broken, I won't mind seeing you again. But you must not pester me to tell tales on your papa, for I shan't do it. And you might as well set that ninny of a Larry's mind at rest, too. Is it true he's to be made a minister?"

"It is spoken of."

"What is this world coming to? Larry Thyrwite sitting in the Cabinet—and Archie Middleton in the Archbishop's Palace!"

"It's in a bad way, all right," he agreed, and left wearing a smile.

There was no sun shining in the sky, but St. Felix felt bathed in a golden glow all the same. It eased his mind that the family was safe from shame and did not trouble him unduly to know what an ass his papa had made of himself over a dumpy little lady with no looks and no sense. Certainly the filling of the thrones of power in the country with idiots did not even occur to him. He thought with satisfaction that the ladies of Upper Grosvenor Square were respectable after all. It pleased him that the younger had been accepted wholeheartedly into Society, and it would have pleased him even more had it been himself who had put the voucher to Almack's into her pocket. But having failed to do that for her, he would see that she did not stray again into any errings ways. What she needed was a wise mentor to point out the pitfalls awaiting the unwary; and of his own wisdom he had not a doubt. His next stop was at Charles Street, to remind his sister to send two tickets to her ball to Mrs. Pealing and her niece. She needed no reminding, but was surprised all the same at his change of sentiment.

"Do they accept this instead of money?" she asked hopefully,

"They don't want anything, Bess. Those two

women have been greatly traduced."

"Turn about is fair play."

"They haven't said a word against anyone and don't intend to."

"Is that the story they are putting about now, that it was all some misunderstanding?"

"It was a misunderstanding. They never actually contacted us or made any demands or threats. We were too previous in our dealing with them."

"Prinney has made the Pealing call off her book. That's what it is. He must be intending to make her his next flirt. It is just as everyone says."

"The lady might have something to say about that," he laughed, but stuck to his vow of silence.

"The one who would have something to say about it is the niece. *She* is the mischief-maker in that nest."

"Beautiful ladies always make mischief, whether they mean to or not," he answered with a soft smile that set his sister's mind to work.

Ten

WITH such great goings-on in London, it was necessary to write and inform the Inglesides. Letters passed in the mail. Sir James warned his daughter to be good and be careful, with Mama adding a postscript to be sure to see if she could find a French *modiste* and not to get her hair cut too short as she read *La Grecque* was to be all the style in the Fall. The Inglesides had each secretly foreseen an unparalleled success for their daughter, but each new letter from her set them reeling, for they had not foreseen such dizzying heights as she was reaching. The Prince of Wales actually taking tea with her and Aunt Effie, and Beau Brummell taking her to parties. "She will be a countess before the Season is out, James, just like Effie," Lady Mary crowed.

"A duchess more like," Sir James replied, his

eyes lighting on the title of the Duke of St. Felix
that cropped up in each letter. The precise nature of
his visits was, of course, not remarked upon.

"Duchess? Your fancy is flying too high, my
dear," Mary chided. Her own had actually soared a
little higher, to the extent of checking the Peerage
to see whether any of the royal dukes were
available.

"And Almack's—that is a good sign. No harm
can come to her at Almack's."

"No, she will have no fun there, but it is well she
was invited," the mother agreed contentedly.

Mrs. Pealing felt that things could hardly have
turned out better had she had a personal communication with God in the heavens. Daphne's visit
was a greater success than she had ever imagined,
or even felt. She herself had money in the bank—a
little, which seemed a lot to her these days. The
Prince of Wales wanted to take her under his
protection, Beau Brummell ran tame at the house,
and now the Duke of St. Felix had as well as said he
was interested in her niece. Her *soirée*, to be held
very soon, would be a wonderful success, for Lady
Melbourne and a dozen of her equals had accepted
most graciously. The triumphs of the present day
were Daphne's driving out with Brummell, to
return home and don a white gown to go to
Almack's with the Wintlocks. It would have been
slightly better had Effie been able to accompany
them, but to know of the triumph was enough for
her. She didn't really like Almack's.

The bright balloon received its first puncture
when Daphne announced blithely that she had no
intention of going to Almack's. "I have given Mrs.

Wintlock the voucher, and she may take Stephanie
if she likes, but I shan't go."

"Why not?" Effie asked, astounded.

"You have told me a dozen times it is a dull old
party."

"What has that to do with anything? It is *the*
place to go. You shall meet everyone and be firm in
your position. It is not to be thought of to stay
away. The patronesses will take it as a personal
insult."

"I don't care if they do. I never wanted to go, and
if they hold themselves too high to invite you, then
I shan't go either." This indeed was half the
reason, but having tried to blackmail St. Felix into
gaining her a voucher, she meant as well to show
him how little value she actually placed on it. If he
had any lingering doubts as to their having been
engaged in blackmail, this must remove it.

Beau Brummell, having heard of the Prince's
morning visit, tried to find out what had tran-
spired when he called for Daphne. Though Mrs.
Pealing had imposed a stricture of silence on St.
Felix, she proved unreticent herself and was soon
pouring into his ears the whole story. He was
vastly disappointed. In his mind the only possible
hitch in the plan was that the Prince would not
come up to scratch. He had never doubted a second
that the silly old lady would snap at the chance to
be taken up by Prinney. His plan of making his
Prince Regent look ridiculous had been thwarted
by this babbling creature, and he was highly vexed
with her. His own sole ambition was to rule
Society, and that anyone in her right mind should
turn down the chance to sit by the reigning

monarch's side was inexplicable to him. In vain he tried to persuade her. He was given to understand the matter was settled. She had turned the Prince of Wales off. She was clearly deranged, and when he was further told that Miss Ingleside, whose wits he had not yet had any occasion to doubt, was not using her voucher to Almack's, he washed his hands of the pair of them. He didn't even take Daphne out for the drive but let on his gouty knee was bothering him. With his own position becoming slippery, he couldn't afford any but respectable friends.

Almack's managed to be entertaining without Miss Ingleside, for her absence caused a lively deal of gossip. The talk was given a nice fillip by the unexpected arrival of the Prince Regent and Mrs. Hertford. Having failed to pick up a new love, Prinney was now anxious to retain the old till he found a suitable replacement. A certain Lady Conyngham was beginning to smile in his direction, but no negotiations were yet underway and he had learned to place no reliance on a smile. Only see how Mrs. Pealing had let him down. He looked lively when Beau Brummell entered, fearing this collapse of his suit with the Pealing was to be laid at his door, but rumours were soon drifting about of a quite different sort.

The Beau was on the outs with her, too, and more especially the niece. What had the silly chit done but refused to come to Almack's because the Patronesses had quite rightly refused a voucher to a divorcée.

"I never heard such gall!" Emily Cowper

announced in injured accents. Her mama, Lady Melbourne, was angry with the Pealing for turning down the Prince. Who would ever believe he had offered? Her spleen was taken out on both of them.

"It was nip and tuck whether we should allow a voucher to Miss Ingleside," Lady Sefton declared, also injured.

"*I* was never consulted on the matter," Mrs. Drummond-Burrell said, "and would have refused a voucher to a young lady making her bows from the home of a divorced woman."

"Quite right!" the Countess de Lieven agreed. "It couldn't be better that she stayed away. She won't have another chance. I think we are agreed on that?"

Agreement was unanimous. Miss Ingleside was to be stricken from the list of Almack's, and she and the Pealing were likewise stricken from the party list of anyone who wished to continue coming to the club. In a night they had tumbled from the very pinnacle of success to the depths of disgrace and didn't even know it. Effie sustained a "feeling" around eleven p.m., but its significance was not explained and she half thought it was heartburn.

. By the time St. Felix arrived with Sir Lawrence and Lady Elizabeth, rather late, and began scanning the room for Miss Ingleside, there was nothing else being discussed but the young lady's brass and the lesson she would be taught. He was her mentor—why had he not gone himself and brought her? What was he doing while she strayed into this perilous path but sitting waiting for Sir Lawrence to prepare a speech he would never make in the House?

"Thank God I haven't mailed the invitations to my ball," Lady Elizabeth said when she heard the story.

St. Felix glared at her. "I see no reason to withhold their invitations only because Beau Brummell has taken them in dislike. We are not to be ruled by a clerk's son, I hope."

"It isn't only Beau. Everyone is saying the same thing. And it is exactly what you said yourself, Dickie. You said we ladies should get together and show them a cold shoulder. Besides, if it's only a travelogue they are writing, Larry won't be in it, for he's never been abroad."

Richard wished to do something to dispel the prevailing mood, which was so strongly anti-Pealing and Ingleside that if the young lady had entered the room at that moment, she would have been cut by everyone except himself. He could see no way in which to help her. Miss Ingleside had flouted an unwritten law in rejecting the invitation. She had implied her disdain of the *ton* and had not even added the sop of pretending illness. She announced boldly to Beau Brummell, of all people, that she stayed away because her aunt was not invited. It couldn't be worse. It would take a miracle to reinstate her, and being only a nominal saint, no miracle was within St. Felix's power.

He left early and went home to consider the matter. Bess had turned coat on him and let him down. She would send no card to her ball when the Patronesses had decreed it was not to be done. He would have to toss a ball himself and haul Mama up from Kent to lend countenance to the ladies. How would Mama take to the idea of his inviting Mrs. Pealing to his ball, with herself to chaperone it? Could he in fairness ask it of her? And would she do it if he did ask? Most importantly of all—for he had answered himself in the affirmative to all his questions—would it work? He left for Kent to find out.

While he plotted and worried and drove to Kent, the town buzzed with their disgrace. And while it buzzed, the ladies, all unaware, planned their gowns for a small party to which they had accepted an invitation the next evening. It was Lady Pamela Thurston to whose home they were invited. She had been one of the first to take up Effie again, after paying her for the diamonds. Lady Pamela was in a state of trepidation bordering on hysteria. Surely they wouldn't *come*! But what if they did? Should she have her butler turn them from the door? If she did anything so rash, might not Effie take it into her head to reveal the past? Borrowing money for the diamonds was not the worst of it. That had been paid back eventually. There was also an interlude with a Mr. Winchester. She was not sure Effie knew a thing about it, but for six months Pamela had been regularly in his company when her husband thought she was paying visits to her sick mama. Effie might know, for Mr. Pealing had been a friend of Mr. Winchester. She dare not turn them from the door—they could ruin her. She dare not let them come in either. She made the clever but cowardly decision to cancel her party, and the awful honour of having the extortionists' company fell to the unwitting Mrs. Deitweiller, who thought herself perfectly safe when Effie had accepted Lady Pamela's invitation.

The Deitweiller do was to be only a small one, but it turned out larger than they thought when Lady Pamela cancelled. Many cards had been sent out to secure a party of forty or so, and with nothing better to do, sixty accepted, half of them at the last minute. That party was to live long in Mrs. Deitweiller's memory as one of the worst days of her life. As the streams of guests kept pouring in, she first worried about refreshments running short; then it was borne in on her that Lady Pamela had called her do off, and why she had done so. From that point on she was on tenterhooks. When Mrs. Pealing and her niece came tapping at the door, the saloon was full to overflowing and buzzing with the latest *on dit* in town—themselves. Their entrance had the effect of a cannon going off in the middle of the Deitweiller room. There was first a stunned silence while every avid eye stared at them. Mrs. Deitweiller, already weak from anticipating this very thing, succumbed to a fainting spell. But in the fraction of a second between seeing them and toppling over, such an expression of horror had been on her face that both the newcomers knew something was terribly amiss. The hostess fallen in a heap on the floor caused some little stir, but only those immediately beside her had their attention torn from the more interesting spectacle of the outcasts receiving their just desserts.

First there was the staring of the crowd to be

endured, then the turning away of every head to find someone else to speak to and pretend not to recognize the newcomers, who looked at each other in helplessness. Mrs. Deitweiller, in a most unappealing state of disarray, was being carried out the door by two footmen and two male guests, and Miss Ingleside, with a rapid recovery from her initial shock, followed them out as though to offer aid to Mrs. Deitweiller. Effie wasn't a terribly swift thinker, but she had enough wits to tag off behind Daphne. Miss Ingleside's intention was to make a hasty exit from the house, but Effie, kinder or less acute, wanted to stay behind to see Mrs. Deitweiller recovered. She had the pleasure of seeing her hostess's eyes open, only to screw up again while she turned her head aside in a moan.

"I'm ruined," Mrs. Deitweiller said, and refused to open her eyes again though she was clearly conscious now.

"Because of our coming?" Daphne asked.

Despite her advanced state of discomposure, the hostess got out a faint "yes."

"Don't fear. We're going," Daphne said, and they did.

"Good gracious me, what was all that about?" Effie asked, while their carriage was brought around.

"There is some new scandal circulating about us," Daphne told her, but she was not able to enlighten her aunt as to the nature of it.

"St. Felix has been up to something," the niece declared.

"St. Felix? No such a thing. When he left me yesterday he was in good spirits and promised to come to call on us again."

"What else could it be? The Prince of Wales calls on you; Beau Brummell has taken us up. Who could have said anything against us?"

"It's that crowd of biddies at Almack's. I knew it was a mistake not to go. A voucher to Almack's is like—it's like a command performance, Daphne. *No one* refuses a voucher."

"I didn't refuse it. I just didn't use it."

"That's probably worse—and never a word to any of them that you were ill."

"I wasn't ill. Would a lie have made it better?"

"Oh, my, yes. That is, it would have made it look better. We must discover what is being said about us."

"If anything *untrue* is being said, the liar will live to regret it," Daphne said in a grim voice.

She had never had any plan of cutting a swathe in Society. Having come to London for a family visit, she had been amused to find herself the center of so much attention, but she suddenly found that while she did not much care for success, she minded total failure very much, indeed. To be stared at by the whole room, as though she were a pariah, and especially to see from the corner of her eye Lady Elizabeth turn away like the rest was unbearable. She had not seen St. Felix—did not believe he had been present—but he would hear from his sister of their rejection and think it served them right.

"The best thing for us to do is to go to Bath or Brighton for a week," Effie decided. "No one will be there yet, but at least it will get us out of town. I can say I'm taking the waters, and there's some money left over, so we can afford it."

"We're not going to run out of town like felons," Daphne said. "We have a card to Mrs. Layton's ball tomorrow night, and you have your party coming up. We can't leave before it."

"There won't be a soul come to it," Effie prophesied glumly. "When the tide turns against you in this city, it turns fast and strong. I've been through this before, you recall. Yesterday we were queens; today we're nobody again."

"Auntie, such chickenheartedness from *you!* After all the scandals you've been through, I should think this would be nothing to you. This is not like your divorce. It is only some little misunderstanding. The thing to do is hold our ground."

"The thing to do is run. I always turn tail and run," Effie admitted shamelessly. "And the only regret I have is that we have no one to help us in our flight. It is much more comfortable if one has a man to run off with. I wonder if St. Felix..."

"Don't you dare suggest such a thing to him!"

"His papa was all for running off with me, love; and really, the young duke is terribly like his papa, only he has no wife, which makes it so much better."

"Not so like his papa that he bothered to call on us, after asking your permission," Daphne reminded her aunt. She had looked forward to seeing him that afternoon, as he had asked permission to call. "He heard the new rumours after leaving us— at Almack's, I suppose—and has deserted us like all the rest."

"It is odd he didn't come," Effie was forced to admit.

St. Felix did not come for the reason that he was

out of town, gone home to the Hall to try to convince his mama to come to town and prop up the reputations of her husband's ex-lover and her niece.

The Dowager Duchess of St. Felix was now sixty-five and no longer given to trotting to London for the Season. She had given it up several years ago and lived a quiet life of retirement in the country, making herself useful to her tenants and local life at large.

"You know I don't bother with balls and routs, Dickie," she explained. She alone was allowed the use of the childish nickname without injunctions from her son. "Bess will be happy to be your hostess, as she always is. Why do you ask me to come?"

"There is a special reason, Mama."

"Is there someone you want me to meet, *at last*?" she asked eagerly.

Between these two, "someone" was understood to mean a prospective bride. "Yes, as a matter of fact, there is."

"Bring her here. We can have a much better visit in the country. Now, sit down and quit that pacing like a tiger and tell me all about her. I suppose she's pretty."

"More than pretty. Beautiful."

"What is her style? Is she a blonde or brunette?"

"She is a brunette, much in the style of the Countess of Standington in her youth, I am given to understand," he said, as an introduction to her identity.

His mother revealed very little trace of emotion, though he discerned a slight blanching of the cheeks. "Oh, yes, she was very pretty. How do you come to know of her, Dickie? She was long before your time."

"The girl is Countess Standington's, now Mrs. Pealing's, niece," he admitted.

"I see," his mother said in a weak voice. "How nice." She looked closely at her son and knew from his quizzing glance that he was aware of at least some part of the truth.

"I know about Papa and Countess Standington," he said. "It is unfortunate, but really, you know, all that past history has nothing to do with Miss Ingleside and myself. I was not aware of it when first I met her."

"Who told you?"

"I had the story from Uncle Algernon," he replied, only half truthfully.

"I didn't know Algie knew. We kept it hushed up as well as we could; but if anyone could weasel it out of your papa, it would be Algie. He was rather sweet on her himself at one time. I don't suppose he told you *that*."

"No, but I suspected as much. Do you dislike the idea very much?" Dickie ventured.

His mother smiled resignedly. "She wasn't the worst lady in the world," she admitted.

"The worst in your view, however, I suppose?"

"I wouldn't say that. Your papa might have fallen into worse clutches. An actress or someone of that sort..."

"Like Perdita, you mean?" Dick suggested with a tentative smile.

"You know that, too, do you? And your father trying so hard to keep all that from you. Well, it wouldn't have been hard to discover. Everyone knew about her. She'd have snapped him up fast enough if he'd ever offered, though of course it was never marriage he had in mind with that one. Countess Standington could have married your papa if she'd wished it. I don't know why she didn't. She loved him, and he was infatuated with her. She might have ruined the reputation of this whole family, and I owe her some debt of gratitude that she chose not to do it. So you are dangling after her niece, eh? The family was good enough. The Countess's father was made an earl when he was quite old. He was only the nephew of Lord Basford and never thought to inherit, but old Basford's son got himself killed in a duel, though they put about it was a hunting accident and her father came into the title. Now, how exactly is Miss Ingleside related to this aunt—is it a direct relationship or through one of her husbands?"

"Mrs. Pealing's sister is her mother. Her father is Sir James Ingleside, a baronet from Wiltshire. Quite unexceptionable, I believe."

"I've heard of the family. But why do you not bring her here, Dickie?"

"That wouldn't do, Mama," he said, and went on to explain the murky waters into which his beloved had pitched herself by her involvement with the aunt's book and her flouting the Patronesses of Almack's.

"The Countess was always a fool, but I never knew her for a demmed fool till this day," the mother said angrily. "How did she come to allow her niece—but it is all of a piece. Why didn't *you* stop her?"

"Have you ever tried to stop a whirlwind?" he asked.

"Like that, is she? She sounds to have a deal more spirit than her aunt. But she has her looks, you say?"

"Others say so. I see absolutely no resemblance myself, and if Daphne ends up looking like that blue-haired lady, I shall divorce or starve her."

"You never mean Effie has run to fat?" the Duchess asked in a joyful tone.

"Fat as a flawn, and her hair dyed blue."

"I am dying to see her," his mother admitted, quite cheered to hear that her competition had aged in so unattractive a fashion. "Very well, I'll go. We'll have the pair to our ball, and Bess must do the same."

"Bess refuses."

"Ha, we'll see if she refuses when I threaten to cut her out of my will. The mother's portion is not entailed, you know," she informed her son.

"Perhaps you would drive with her—Daphne, I mean—in the Park and let it be seen she has your approval. I think that would bring the Castlereaghs and possibly Lady Melbourne and a few of the *grande dames* into line."

"Bess and Lawrence must be made to toe the line. They are more connected with Society these days than I am."

For an hour the two sat with their heads together discussing tactics, and when Richard left, his mama immediately set her abigail to packing trunks for a longish sojourn in the city. She'd go early and be there for Bess's ball, too, as she was to make the devilish trip anyway. The Duchess of St.

Felix went to her mirror and observed her face with an intensity she had not bothered with in years. She had not aged so badly. She wished her husband were alive today to see his beloved countess turned to fat and blue hair, while his wife, whom he had never half appreciated, retained a good, straight, thin figure and hair that was still black at the back, though the front had turned a nasty salt-and-pepper colour. She knew George had never loved her, but he was a sensible man as a rule, and she had been shocked when he said he meant to leave her. He had been temporarily insane and Dickie was clearly in the same state. Best to go along with him, or heaven only knew what folly he would commit.

The lack of letters to Wiltshire following this episode in the eventful visit to London was put down to the rigours of the Season, but the rigours were not of the sort imagined.

"Very likely she is off to some great country house for a visit with Brummell and the Prince of Wales and is too busy to write," Lady Mary sighed happily. The absence of communication was an excellent omen. Effie had never written much when she was busy with her great friends.

Sir James looked at her and shook his head. "No, it is this St. Felix that has got her head in such a whirl she forgets to write to us. I have been checking on him—he has an excellent character. Related to the Archbishop of Canterbury."

"He can't help that, dear," Lady Mary consoled him. "There are clergymen in every family if you dig deep enough. Why, I have a second cousin who is a dean in London, and your younger nephew is studying to take orders."

"Thirty years old—just the right age," Sir James continued.

"Only fancy Beau Brummell giving Effie a blue rose," Mary rambled on. "I hope she kept it to press."

James realized it was pointless talking to his wife.

Eleven

E FFIE stuck to her guns that the only course open to Daphne and her was to run off to Bath. A careful reckoning of her bank account, coupled with the fact that Prinney's holiday Pavilion being at Brighton might take the social set there, had tipped the scales in Bath's favour. Daphne was resolved they should stay in London and brazen it out. She spoke repeatedly of their own party and at last convinced Effie that they should remain in the city till that date was past.

"Nobody will come," Effie warned her niece. "But we'll stay close to the house in the meantime and prepare for it as though it were to take place. Such a waste of food, but I shan't order much. Just one or two dozen lobsters and a case of champagne, and I must have Cook make up chantillies for the ladies. Such a sad, scrambling do. I used to throw much finer parties in the old days. There was never a lack of guests. Everyone begged to be let in and went to such shifts to wangle a card."

"If we are to rusticate in Bath, I shall want to take some books with me," Daphne decided.

"My dear, there is a fine circulating library there, on Milsom Street. But what you must do is notify Mrs. Wintlock you are leaving town. Odd she hasn't come by before this."

"She has been cross with me ever since I refused to go to Almack's. She did not like to take Stephanie when it was myself the vouchers were given to. I told her I have a cold."

"I wish you had told the Patronesses the same thing. That would have saved all this bother of preparing for a party that ain't going to take place."

"It will take place, if you and I have to sing and dance with each other."

"That is just what we will be doing, I have no doubt. I think St. Felix might come, if you would let me give him a card."

"What, when he has never done a thing to entertain us but come here and complain? I should think not. You gave his sister one, and we shall see whether she makes any use of it. She turned her cheek on us, like all the others at the Deitweiller's party."

After a moment's silence, Daphne reverted to her interest in taking some books with her despite the excellent library at Bath. Her real aim was to get on to Bond Street and gauge exactly how violent was the reaction against herself and Effie. Meeting people in singles or twosomes might be more friendly than confronting a whole roomful. If it seemed possible that some of their friends were still friends, she hoped to remind them of the party and try by degrees to reestablish herself and Effie. "I like to read in the carriage," she said. "It will be a long trip, and reading helps to pass the time."

"You'll burn out your eyes trying to read in a jostling carriage with no light."

"I always read in the carriage," Daphne persisted untruthfully.

"You can read the memoirs then."

"I was hoping to get Byron's *Hebrew Melodies*."

"Oh, well, if you know exactly what you want, it's no problem. I'll send a boy down to Hookham's Library for it."

"No! No, I also want some fresh air. You have gone to the expense of hiring a team, and we may as well have some use from them. They have not been out of the stable these two days."

Effie saw that her niece meant to show her face on Bond Street come hell or high water and finally gave in to the extent of accompanying her in the carriage, though she would not dismount. They passed more than one carriage whose occupants were known to them, but no friendly waves were exchanged. "I told you how it would be," Effie said glumly. When they reached Hookham's, Effie remained in the carriage as she had said she would and Daphne was obliged to go alone into the library to procure her copy of the *Hebrew Melodies*, a duplicate of which sat at home on her dresser in Wiltshire.

As she started to enter the shop, she recognized Lady Pamela's orange hair coming towards her.

The lady turned abruptly and crossed the street, very nearly throwing herself under a passing carriage in her haste to get away from Miss Ingleside. Daphne was angry when she entered the place. She looked around her briskly to see whether she recognized anyone. She did not, which was fortunate as her temper might well have induced her to some impertinence. She was in no hurry to make her selection but, in fact, was determined to dawdle till someone she knew came in. For ten minutes she leafed through volumes in which she had not the least interest, after which she decided she was wasting her time and left without taking a single book. She was about to step into the waiting carriage when she noticed a small group collected on the street in front of a different shop.

"Hurry up!" Effie called out to her, and as she was on the point of entering, Effie explained the reason for haste. "There's Lady Melbourne and the Beau looking into that window. We must get away before they spot us."

"How uncivil you are become. I must say hello to Beau," Daphne replied and walked to the window that had attracted the crowd, while Effie's heart sank.

Cartoons and short verses were being put on display, and the mob was surging forward to see the latest lampoon of their Prince Regent. He was depicted by the satirical cartoonist Cruikshank as sitting on a fat cushion amidst the splendid chinoiserie of one of his many saloons, holding court while fawning courtiers, all in kimonos, bowed to him.

"He hasn't a chance of recovering from this," Lady Melbourne said.

"I think he has caught the essence of our Regent rather well," Beau drawled, holding up his glass to take in all details and see what might make him think of a sharp comment.

"Good afternoon, Lady Melbourne, Mr. Brummell," Daphne said, smiling at them boldly.

They both looked at her in amazement, and after exchanging a glance, they both nodded coolly and said not a word.

"Cat got your tongue, Mr. Brummell?" Daphne asked, her ire rising. "Lady Melbourne, have you stolen Mr. Brummell's tongue?" Lady Melbourne's eyes bulged in shock, but Daphne had already turned back to Beau.

"I should have thought that with Mr. Cruikshank's cartoon to inspire you, you might get off a witty word against the Prince. But I see I catch you unprepared. Those spontaneous epigrams of yours require some thinking about."

Beau admired her style and brass in spite of himself. To call Lady Melbourne a cat was famous. "Actually it was the short verses, reputed to be by Lord Byron, that we were perusing," he said. No brilliant words came to him regarding the cartoon. "I see he has honoured me with a quatrain."

"And his dog with another," Daphne commented, glancing at the squibs.

"We must be going," Lady Melbourne said to her escort, but the Beau was not to let her slur go unchallenged.

"Are you unescorted, Miss Ingleside? It is not the custom for a young *lady* to walk the streets alone in London."

"I have reason to know one is never safe in London. When her friends cut her, what is to be expected of strangers?"

"You must be careful whom you recognize here," he returned with something close to a sneer.

"Yes, especially when your own social position is so tenuous," she said sharply.

"We really must be off," Lady Melbourne remarked, taking hold of Beau's arm. "Nice chatting with you, Miss Ingleside."

"No hurry, dear Lady Melbourne," Mr. Brummell said, patting her hand. "*My* position, and your own, of course, permit us even to speak a moment to Miss Ingleside without fear of falling into anonymity. Did you enjoy the Deitweiller's rout last night, Ma'am? One hears you were there—for a moment."

"Yes, we could only spare them a minute for we are very busy. You may have heard we are engaged in writing a book."

"So I've heard. Am *I* to be one of your victims?"

"No, we are only writing about highly placed and famous people. Good day, Mr. Brummell, Lady Melbourne." She curtsied and walked away before he had time to retort.

"What a bold minx it is," Brummell laughed to his companion. "I really regret that that girl has sunk herself. I should enjoy crossing swords with her again."

"I can't think why. You always get the worst of it," Lady Melbourne roasted him.

"You didn't distinguish yourself, *Cat*. I am out of practice. With her for a sparring partner I would improve." He turned back to Cruikshank's cartoon. "What do we think of this?" he asked.

"We are amused. It is quite like him."

"That won't sound well at the clubs. We want more panache. Shall we declare that having outgrown his father's throne, he is now occupying the floor? And looking very much at home there, too."

At the carriage Effie enquired fearfully what had occurred between her niece and the pair at the window. "Just commenting on the display," Daphne told her, but the sparks shooting from the girl's eyes belied her mild answer.

"I don't suppose Beau mentioned anything about our party? I know Lady Melbourne won't come."

"He didn't mention it," Daphne said, but in her heart she knew there was to be no redemption through the party. Their curtness told her clearly that she and Effie were through, and she became resigned to skulking off to Bath, where she was beginning to think they ought to spend the rest of her visit, with the two of them going to Wiltshire at its termination.

She began assembling her belongings from all the corners of the apartment and was just asking to have her trunks hauled up from the cellar when Effie came to her door. "It's St. Felix," her aunt said, smiling brightly.

"What does he want?" Daphne asked.

"He wants to see you."

"I don't want to see him. Tell him I am too busy."

"I'll do no such thing. Comb your hair and go

say how-do-you-do, at least."

Daphne was reluctant to face Lord St. Felix in the midst of her disgrace, yet she also felt a strong urging to run down to the Blue Saloon as fast as her legs could carry her. "I suppose I must say hello as he is come," she said and brushed out her curls in preparation for the meeting.

When she entered the room, she said, "You must excuse the mess. I was busy upstairs. We have not been receiving callers the past few days."

"You would have received a call from me yesterday had I been in town," he answeed.

"Oh, I didn't realize you had been away," she said. She wondered then if he knew of her disgrace. She had not been at Almack's, and he had not been at the Deitweiller do. To discover whether his sister might have told him of the latter, she asked if he had been to see Lady Elizabeth.

"No, I came here directly I got back from Kent," he said. "In fact, I haven't been to my own house yet." He still wore a many-caped driving coat.

This seemed like an undue eagerness for her company. "Is there a particular reason for this call?" she enquired.

"Yes, a most particular one. I want to find out how things are going, after the fiasco at Almack's the other night."

"Oh, you were there! We—that is—I did not attend. I'm afraid my absence might have caused a little talk."

"Particularly as you made no excuse but announced—to Brummell of all people!—that you stayed away because of your aunt not receiving a voucher. You must know a divorcée is not welcome there."

"They draw the line at bigamists! The Prince..."

He waved away her objection. "Prinney is a law unto himself."

"As a divorcée is my best friend and aunt and hostess, I did not choose to go either."

"You couldn't leave well enough alone!" he charged angrily and threw his driving coat on a chair. "Having achieved the impossible and got yourself invited, you must thumb your nose at the world and snub everyone who matters in town. Good God, what am I going to do with you!"

"Say goodbye, if you like. We are leaving for a holiday in Bath."

"No, that's the wrong move. If you run now we'll never be able to hold up our heads."

"We?" she asked in astonishment. "*You* are not involved in our disgrace. It has nothing to do with you."

"It has a great deal to do with me. I consider Mrs. Pealing as a sort of surrogate mother. You recall telling me she might almost have been my mother. She was extremely kind in all her dealings with my family, and I wish to repay her."

"She never had any intention of publishing that story or any of the others she could if she wished it. You know that was all a misunderstanding."

"Oh, publishing—I forgot all about that. I referred to the duel, and the suicide threat, and so on."

"You mean she told you the whole thing, and

she made *me* promise not to!"

"It slipped out. She was not *bragging* about it, if that is your fear."

"Yes, slipped out, while you put a dozen sly questions to her. Well, it serves you right if you found out what you didn't want to hear."

"Certainly it does, but that is of no importance now. I don't consider your situation hopeless by any means."

"You don't know the worst of it," she warned.

"What else have you been up to? More chicanery?" he asked with foreboding.

"We were so foolhardy as to accept an invitation we received to a small rout."

"You shouldn't have, not after the scrape at Almack's. Let's hear all about it. Cut dead by half the group there, I imagine."

"No, by all of it, with the hostess herself falling into a fainting fit at our feet."

He swallowed uneasily and asked, "Where did this take place? Not at one of the better homes I trust?"

"Deitweillers."

He considered the name and seemed unsure whether to include it amongst the better homes. "Who was there?"

"Your sister, for one. Our visit was so brief I hadn't much chance to notice."

"We may manage to keep it quiet."

"Oh, no, we are too notorious for that, Aunt Effie and I. It is quite the talk in the city today. Brummell mentioned it to me." Daphne was unsure why she was telling all this to St. Felix. Her most ardent wish had been that he never hear a word of it, but once he was there in person the whole came tumbling out. He would desert them like the others, and she wanted to have her fate sealed once for all, that she might get on with making a new life.

"Ah, still on terms with the Beau, are you? That's good."

"You said he didn't matter! You said he was on the verge of ruin!"

"He may go on being on the verge for a year. He isn't done for yet. I'm glad you have retained his friendship."

"I haven't retained it! I insulted him just this afternoon."

"Oh, lord, can you *never* keep that tongue of yours between your teeth! What happened?"

She gave him some idea of their conversation, and he shook his head at her folly. "He's out then. And Lady Melbourne was with him, you say?"

"Yes, and she hardly let on to recognize me at all. She wouldn't have spoken if Brummell hadn't been goaded into exchanging insults with me. The situation is clearly hopeless, and Auntie and I mean to hide our heads in shame at Bath, after which I must find some weapon to beat Papa into accepting her at home. But you needn't look so distressed. Auntie gave up on Society years ago, and I never thought to set up as an Incognita at all when I came. Once I am home, all this unpleasant interlude will be soon forgotten. I am not ruined, you know, not in Wiltshire, in any case, and that is where I belong. I shall make a very good match in spite of all this tempest in a teapot here."

"You would give me to understand you have all

the country beaux at your beck and call?"

"But, of course. Did you doubt it for a minute?"

"No, but I think you can do better than a country beau. Have you no desire to revenge yourself on those who have calumniated you?" he asked in a leading fashion.

"I would adore it if Auntie would publish every scandalous story she knows, but she is too sweet-tempered to even take offence at the Turkish treatment she has received. It is her decision to go to Bath, and I come to think she is right."

"Well, I do not. You will both remain in London, and you will come to Bess's ball next week."

"It is *naturally* our first aim to do as you say, but there is a difficulty. We have not received invitations, you see."

"You will."

"It is very kind of you to wish to redeem your surrogate mother's reputation, but you exert yourself to no purpose. We have gone beyond redemption and mean to run and hide in Bath."

"When did you plan to leave?"

"In a few days' time." She didn't mention their pending party.

"Don't be in a hurry. I'll see you again before you leave. I am having a ball myself and had hoped to coerce you to come to it."

"Now there is a change. It is not long since you were trying to coerce me *not* to attend your sister's tea party. Neither face nor form did you wish to darken her door."

"I hope I have more luck this time. What I ought to be doing is threatening to beat you if you come," he said, smiling in a way he had not smiled at her before. There was something intimate in this look.

"Yes, it's clear your actual aim is to keep us away at all costs, and you know the likeliest way to achieve it is to pretend you desire our presence."

"But I *do* desire your presence, Miss Ingleside. Face and form are both welcome. Did I *really* say that?"

"Indeed you did, and a great many other rude things. I have them all carefully jotted down in my memoirs, for the epilogue."

"Do you have jotted down as well how you goaded me on to it? I was never in your company once that you were not tweaking me."

"And how beautifully you responded to every pinch!"

"You have been leading me on to make an ass of myself from the day we met. You could have told me your aunt had no intention of printing any of those stories."

"I told you a dozen times, or tried to, but I soon perceived there was no telling a St. Felix anything."

"You can tell me something I want to know. Where exactly in Wiltshire do you reside?"

"Near Trowbridge. Just a hop away from Bath. We might stop in at home en route."

"What is your father's place called?"

"Ingleside Manor. Why do you wish to know?"

"I like to know where my friends come from."

"You don't mean to say I still have a friend? And the one person, too, I would have sworn was an enemy."

"Oh, no, I never make an enemy of a beautiful lady if I can help it."

"Next you will be telling me I have a charming disposition!" she laughed, surprised and very well pleased at the compliment.

"You base that on the assumption that love is blind, no doubt; but you will remember I have eyes to see you are beautiful, and they also show me clearly that you have the disposition of a termagant."

"What a disappointment! I have not made a conquest after all, then?" she quizzed.

"You haven't half exerted yourself, Miss Ingleside," he replied and arose to pick up his driving coat.

"No more have you."

"No, I have been too busy trying to hate you." His warm smile told her how little he had succeeded. "Good day."

He was gone, and Miss Ingleside sat looking at the empty doorway, wondering if he meant what she thought.

It was clear, in any case, that he meant to help her and Aunt Effie regain their footing in London society. James's daughter was ready to get her back up at any offer of help, but there was enough of her mother, or perhaps just feminine nature, in her that she did not totally disdain the offer to share her burdens with such an eager young man. In fact, she thought the main difference between herself and Effie was that her aunt wanted the help of a man to engineer a comfortable escape, while she welcomed the offer of one to help her stay and fight. She felt some fear that the man in question meant to have things very much his own way. "That's the wrong move." "You will both remain in London." Never a question, but bald assertions and commands. He was the sort who would *tell* a girl she was going to marry him, not ask her. The considering frown that puckered her brow faded, and a smile settled on her lips as she pondered these faults on the part of Lord St. Felix.

But despite his faults, she felt the need of guidance from him or someone like him. He had said she shouldn't have come to London alone, and he was right. She had accidentally achieved an early success, but inexperience of city ways had nearly undone her; and if St. Felix could and would set her on the right path, she would do what she could to go along with him. Aunt Effie meant well, but she was neither wise nor strict enough to be a good guide.

Twelve

ST. Felix's next stop, even before going home, was to Charles Street to see Bess. He found her at home but had to wait out the departure of some callers.

"You have to send cards to Mrs. Pealing and her niece for your ball," he said as soon as they were alone.

"It is impossible, Dickie."

"Call me Richard, if you please."

"Yes, well, it is still impossible. What has the silly girl done now but go barging into a party the very night after not going to Almack's, and there was never such a sight, Richard. Mrs. Deitweiller fell over in a swoon, and the two of them trailed out the room after her, happy for any excuse to leave for everyone was snickering."

"Very civilized behaviour, I'm sure; and yourself amongst the snickerers, Bess?"

"No one could keep a straight face. We were all hoping they'd come back in, but they hadn't the gall for that. What can have gotten into them to attend?"

"An attack of innocence, I expect. Miss Ingleside wouldn't know the seriousness of the Almack's affair, and Mrs. Pealing is not so bright as one could wish in her chaperone."

"But you can't expect me to have a repeat of the Deitweiller rout!"

"No, I expect much better behaviour from you than fainting in shock. You will make them welcome and see they are introduced."

"Are they threatening to print that story about Larry again? Is that it?"

"No, they are not," he said curtly.

"Then why are you trying to make me ask them here? You know it will be fatal to Larry's chances; and for myself, I should prefer the company of the rest of London to theirs."

"You will have both."

"I can't do it. If it weren't for Larry I would, but at this *crucial* time in his career..."

"It will look very bad indeed for Larry if his own brother-in-law cannot recommend him for the Ministry," he said in an offhand way.

Bess was instantly on her feet. "Dickie, you wouldn't! That *is* blackmail."

"So it is. I have learned a trick from Mrs. Pealing."

"Why are you so anxious for them to be accepted? They are nothing to us."

"They are something to *me.* I have become very interested in them."

"I see what it is! They're blackmailing you about that woman being Papa's flirt. I have been thinking about that, and I don't think they can prove it."

"That is not why I'm doing it."

"Why, then?"

"For Larry," he said in a kindly voice.

"You said they weren't going to print that."

"They are not, but only think how ill it would look for my wife to be cut by the whole city. It would be bound to reflect on Larry's position—and promotion—don't you think?"

"Dickie, you have never *married* that creature!"

"No, I haven't even written to her father yet, and in future I would prefer if you refer to Miss Ingleside as a lady, rather than a creature. I only knew his direction a half hour ago and am about to write to him now. I don't foresee any difficulty. So, for the sake of Larry, I really think we ought all to stick together and make Society accept Miss Ingleside and her aunt."

"Oh, my dear, yes. What will Mama say when she hears? This will kill her, Richard, and I don't know how you can be *so* unfeeling."

"She has heard, and what she says is that if you wish to inherit anything from her, you will ask Mrs. Pealing and Miss Ingleside to your ball. She comes to mine herself, by the by."

"How did you have the nerve to tell her you mean to marry that woman's niece?"

"It took every atom of mettle I possess, but she didn't take it half badly. Papa might have fared worse at Perdita's hands, you see. That was the saving crumb."

"Perdita who?" Bess asked, her mind reeling from so much bad news.

"Perdita, Mrs. Robinson. Papa's other flirt. You are old enough to remember Perdita."

Bess sank back on the sofa, wilted. "Go away, Dickie. I have had more than enough bad news for one day," she said in a failing voice. "I'll just sit here and succumb quietly to a fit of the vapours."

"Have a feather burned under your nose. Might I suggest that particularly ugly pink one you had stuck in your hair like an Indian at the opera last week?"

She glared at him. "Maybe they won't come. That is my only hope."

"They'll come if I have to truss them up in ropes and drag them here. I'll need some help organizing *my* ball, as well. I'll drop by tomorrow and talk to you about it."

"You'll put in a good word for Larry with Liverpool?" she regained enough strength to ask.

"But, of course. Families must stick together. I'll threaten to turn Whig if they don't give him a folio."

"Oh, would you, Dickie?"

"No, but Richard might, if you ask him very nicely. I begin to perceive this blackmail is a handy weapon."

"And I always thought you were so good."

"Where did you get such a cork-brained notion as that?" he asked, and left the room laughing.

Effie and Daphne received the invitation,

delivered in person the next morning by St. Felix, who urged an acceptance on them. They demurred, disliking to go again into Society after their recent ignominy. St. Felix had other proposals to put forward, as well. Invitations to drive in the Park and to let him escort them to the opera were fended off with sundry weak excuses. He had no luck in any of these lesser plans, but he felt them to be weakening in their resolve not to attend the ball. Effie was not much good at resisting any scheme urged on her more than once; and Miss Ingleside, though recalcitrant, secretly wanted very much to go to the ball. She felt also that if St. Felix insisted, it was the right thing to do. So he bided his time, since he was not sure in his own mind that a too hasty re-entry on the scene was wise, while always putting forward a mention of their attending Bess's ball.

He came daily to Upper Grosvenor Square to amuse the ladies, and with such agreeable entertainment on the premises, excursions beyond the apartment were hardly missed. Effie read to them from the memoirs, and for one whole rainy afternoon the three of them browsed through the diaries, discussing old scandals, while Effie clucked a warning they were not to repeat a word of it.

"Prinney and Mrs. Abercrombie!" St. Felix asked wide-eyed, and demanded confirmation that it was the same Mrs. Abercrombie who would not allow her daughters to go to plays or ridottos.

"To be sure it is. I have often remarked it is the mothers who most ran wild themselves who keep a tight rein on their own daughters. I daresay if *I* had ever had one, she'd have ended up in a convent."

"And seduced every monk for miles around!" St. Felix gibed.

"Just like his father," Effie said to Daphne with a rueful shake of her head.

Effie was neither wise nor clever, but if she knew anything she knew the machinations of romance, and she sat with a gloating look as she thought to herself what an excellent *parti* she had found for Daphne. She noticed with satisfaction that till Daphne entered the room St. Felix's eyes were never far from the door, and when she was in it, they were not often anywhere but on her. If she arose to get a book or paper, he followed her every movement, and even if she sat reading quietly, he would watch her for minutes at a time without saying a word, as if he were bewitched. Maybe he was—his father had said *she'd* bewitched him. If it hadn't been for Standington—such a fine figure of a man—things might have turned out very differently.

He did a deal of complaining, too, like his papa. Daphne was growing pale from not being out— and her cheeks blooming like a rose. She was too thin—wasn't she losing weight?—and her gowns fitting her to a "T," just the way they fit when she arrived.

"Time will take care of the latter," Daphne informed him casually. "My family runs to plumpness."

"He cast a surreptitious eye in Effie's direction and asked, "Really?" in an uneasy tone.

"Don't believe a word of it!" Effie assured him, wondering what maggot had got into Daphne's head. "Her mama is thin as a rail."

"You haven't seen her in years, Auntie. She is pleasingly plump these days."

"She must have shrunk to a midget, then, for she told me in her last letter she weighs just over eight stone."

"And a rouge pot will look after my pallor," Daphne added.

"Ladies shouldn't paint!" St. Felix objected at once. "Except—except ladies who are no longer in the first blush of youth," he added to Effie, whose natural high colour did not look quite natural. And, of course, he knew no one's eyelids were blue.

"Pooh—if I weren't as pink as a peony already, *I'd* paint," Effie told him. "You men are all alike. Arthur never liked me to wear a drop of paint on my eyes or a thing, but he liked it well enough on the actresses. *They* may use all the tricks to make themselves attractive and steal our husbands from us, but *we* are not to paint or curl our hair or squeeze into a corset in case another man takes a look at us. They want their mistresses to look pretty, but not their wives. I don't know what they can be thinking about. And if you're foolish enough to listen to them, they'll turn right around and tell you to smarten yourself up and quit looking like a dowd. It makes no sense to me, and I never minded what Arthur said in the matter but put paint on my eyelids like Mrs. Jordan. She taught me how to do it so it didn't look unnatural."

"Did Mrs. Jordan use blue paint?" St. Felix

asked, making himself very much at home.

"No, she used green, but one of Arthur's lightskirts used blue. I got the trick of surrounding myself with blue from her. Her name was Gloxinia. She had a wardrobe of blue, and even a carriage."

"Shame on you, Auntie. It is a trick worthy of a mistress," Daphne said without looking anywhere in the direction of St. Felix, even when she heard him clear his throat quite audibly.

He was invited to remain for lunch on this occasion, making the cubbyhole of a dining parlour seem even smaller. The finest tableware was again on display, and the meal a happy one. In spite of this, or because of it, Daphne found her appetite flagging. She refused the pigeon pie first, then the ham.

"You must eat something," St. Felix told her in the stern accents of a father.

"I'll eat dessert," she said, a remark that always goaded her papa into an exhortation on the high cost of food and the crime of wasting it.

"It seems a shame to wate all this good meat and vegetables," St. Felix said, scowling at her. From having imagined her to be losing weight, he had quit worrying about her filling out to Effie's size.

"Yes, and with food costing so much, too!" she replied with a twinkle in her eyes.

"No one can live on sweets," he declared, and passed along a bowl of peas, which were declined with polite thanks. "You haven't eaten a bit! Effie—Mrs. Pealing—is this the way she always eats?"

"No, indeed, she has a hearty appetite usually."

Bread, butter, and a plate of sweetmeats were

sent down the table, and all refused, for by this time Daphne saw he meant to have his way and would not eat a bite till the dessert came, if she starved to death in the meantime. St. Felix grew more impatient by the minute, and when at last dessert came, he said, "If you have no appetite for nourishing food, you shouldn't stuff yourself with cake."

"If I don't eat my meat and potatoes I can't have a treat?" she asked, laughing. "How very like home it is. Papa used to say so when I was a child."

"If a young lady behaves like a child, she must be treated like one."

"Oh, no! That is the best part of being grown up. We may do as we please, and overbearing adults can do no more than frown and fuss, for they would not be so rag-mannered as to *tell* us we are behaving childishly." She looked boldly at her would-be father, who first stared back at her, then laughed reluctantly.

"Don't try to turn me into a father, young lady."

"I am trying to prevent you from becoming one, or from becoming mine, in any case."

"I have no intention of being a father to you."

"That's good. One is quite enough when he is so much a father as mine is."

"James is a father and a mother," Effie explained to their guest, and gave a dozen examples of each role, with a few animadversions on Arthur's similar manner of treating herself.

A few days passed in this pleasant manner, and when Effie's party rolled around, not a single visitor came to attend it. They did not invite St. Felix, not for fear he would stay away, but for fear he would come and be the only guest. The two of them ate as much lobster and chantilly and drank as much champagne as they could hold in an attempt to be merry, but the pervading atmosphere was one of darkest gloom.

"How can we possibly show our faces at a ball, when no one comes to us?" Daphne asked. "Even Lady Elizabeth didn't come."

She would have done had her brother known anything of the matter, but in his ignorance he didn't push her to it, and she had enough sense not to mention it to him. She hoped her absence would give the ladies the hint they were not overly welcome at her ball, but as the important evening drew near, she received their acceptances. St. Felix had wheedled and cajoled them out of an immediate remove to Bath, and, as they were in London with so little to do, they were eventually talked into accepting the invitation. Neither lady was completely happy about it, and it would have taken no more than a sniffle for them both to call off; but no sniffle or sneeze befriended them, and when the day of the ball dawned bright and clear and healthy, they sat together over breakfast, inquiring minutely into each other's condition.

"We could say our gowns aren't ready," Daphne suggested.

"Mine wants hemming," Effie offered, ready to grasp at any weak little straw.

"He'll be here before noon to see we mean to go through with it," Daphne cautioned, hoping for a stronger excuse.

During his recent visits to the apartment, he had become such a dictator in the matter of the ball that a better pretext than an unhemmed gown in mid-morning was called for.

"I'll tell him I feel a fever coming on," Effie decided.

Daphne looked at her askance. "You'll have to stay in your room then and let me tell him, or put flour on your cheeks. You are blooming, Auntie."

"I don't feel at all well," the aunt replied. "It's the fever that's making me pink."

They both sat on in silence, their minds working hard at an excuse that might pass muster with the dictator. "I feel positively *unwell*," Effie repeated a moment later.

"You," Daphne began, then stopped, for Aunt Effie no longer looked fine. She had turned stark, bone white. "Oh—not a *feeling*! Wild horses wouldn't drag me to this ball if you have a premonition about it. There is some horrid surprise in store for us, I know it. I think I feel it myself."

"There's something in the air all right," Effie said, as the first jolt of her feeling passed off.

"Has it to do with the ball?" Daphne demanded, a firm believer in her aunt's supernatural powers.

A little smile hovered around Effie's lips and her colour returned. "No, I don't think so," she answered. It was—it was Arthur, dear," she said.

"You had an intimation he was coming before, but he never showed."

"No, I only felt he was *thinking* about me before, but now I feel he is coming."

"What about the ball? That doesn't tell us what we should do about that. Try to have a feeling about it, Effie."

Effie obediently closed her eyes and tried to gain

a sensation regarding the ball, but she drew a blank. "I don't feel a thing," she announced after a few moments. "I just can't picture us there at all, but that doesn't mean we shan't go. These feelings come of their own accord. I had no warning of the Deitweiller do, you remember? Sometimes I know what's going to happen and sometimes I don't. It's extremely annoying, but it's a gift, you know." This satisfied her as to any vagaries in the matter, and she lifted up the *Morning Observer* to see what was new in the world.

She read aloud a few items of little interest to herself and none to her niece, but failed to find mention that Lord Standington was come to England, which was what she was really looking for. She was about to lay the paper aside when her eyes suddenly darted back to a notice. "What's this?"

"What is it?" Daphne echoed her.

"The Dowager Duchess of St. Felix is come up from Kent, paying a visit to her family at Belgrave Square. Daphne, St. Felix's wife is in town!"

"His mother, you mean. This is the end. We can't possibly go to Lady Elizabeth's ball if *she* is to be there. St. Felix knew nothing of this when he urged us to attend. It would be quite improper for *you* to go, and I obviously can't go alone. We'll tell him when he comes. He is sure to understand." The looked-for excuse had been found but brought a woeful sense of letdown with it. The day, to have been busy with preparations for the ball, now yawned before them with nothing to brighten it.

"Thank God for that," Effie said, better pleased than her niece.

Another letdown was in store for Miss Ingleside.
St. Felix, who had spent nearly as much time with
them lately as he spent at his own home or
anywhere else, did not come. It did not occur to the
ladies that he might be busy running around town
performing last-minute chores for his sister's ball
and his mother's attendance at it. They did receive
two corsages from him to be worn for the occasion.
Both were put in vases to set in the Blue Saloon as
a constant reminder that they would not be worn.
Daphne was completely in the dumps, but her aunt
was not aware of it. She went ahead with all
preparations for a *grande toilette* despite its
having been firmly established between them that
they were not going to attend the ball.

"There is no saying what might happen before
the day's out," Aunt Effie smiled happily, and had
the hair dresser do her hair in an elaborate style
that Daphne suspected was copied from Gloxinia,
for it managed to be both vulgar and old-
fashioned. It required only the sticking on of two
ostrich feathers to be ready for anything.

"Get yours done up, too, love. You don't know
where you might end up this night," Effie pleaded.

"We'll end up right in this Blue Saloon, and I
don't mean to give myself a headache for that."
She spent a long, tiring afternoon sitting with a
book in her lap, looking out the window and
waiting for a visit from St. Felix, who in some
magical manner was to make it not only possible
for her to go to his sister's ball with Aunt Effie but
impossible for her not to. When the afternoon wore
on and still he did not come, she began seeking
reasons for it. His mama's arrival had made it

impossible for them to go, and he was ashamed to come and tell them so. He counted on their discretion to stay away. That she had never displayed a jot of discretion in any of her other dealings with him was forgotten. She knew he was aware of their subscribing to the *Observer* and their addiction to the social column since they had attended those few parties. He had not mentioned asking his mother to hostess his own ball, so Daphne had no way of realizing his feelings in the matter. He was quite clearly hinting them away.

While Miss Ingleside suffered her tedious vigil, Effie bustled about in a state near euphoria. She hummed off key all day long, driving her niece to the edge of distraction. Her blue eyes glowed, her pink cheeks bloomed, and her hair, freshly tinted by the coiffeur, positively gleamed. She babbled on that it was fortunate they had so much champagne left over from the party, for Arthur liked it excessively. It was a pity the lobster couldn't have been saved, too, but she had Cook run out for a large saddle of mutton. A dozen times she congratulated herself for having had the front room done over and looked happily at the new acquisitions. When dinner-time came, she told the servants to lay three places.

"Who is coming?" Daphne enquired eagerly, wondering with a lift of elation if St. Felix was to join them and she had in some manner not been informed of it.

"There is no saying when he will get here," Effie told her.

"Who?" Daphne asked, smiling herself now.

"Arthur, my dear. I *told* you about my feeling at breakfast. He is coming; I know it."

Daphne's faith in her aunt's powers was sinking, as was her faith in everything at the tagend of this interminable day. "Don't pin too much hope on it," she advised.

"No, to be sure I am not, love. I'll just tell Cook to make sure she puts on an extra serving of green peas, for Arthur was always fond of them."

The third place went unoccupied when the ladies finally sat down to dinner. The extra peas were wasted, and a bottle of champagne half drunk without a single compliment on its excellence. It might have been vinegar for all the note either of them took of it. They returned to the Blue Saloon to resume waiting for what Daphne was now convinced was to be nothing more exciting than a cup of tea and a hand of piquet before going to bed. The only difference from their early evenings together was that Effie was dressed as fine as five pence in a blue crepe gown, fingering two blue ostrich feathers, sitting on the very edge of a chair and jumping a foot at every rattle of windows or sound of a carriage passing in the streets.

The clock chimed nine, and even Effie's ebullience began to wear thin. "Is it possible he's not coming?" she asked, genuinely perplexed.

"I'm afraid it is not only possible but certain," Daphne said. No sooner were the words out than there was a footfall on the front step, followed by a tapping of the knocker. The ladies looked at each other. Each was sure the caller was for herself and felt a little sorry for the other. While they sat looking and breathing faster, the butler announced Lord Standington, and into the room stepped a little leprechaun of a man not quite five feet tall, with sharp black eyes and a flying wisp of white hair, much longer on one side than the other, till he felt it tickle his ear, and with a swipe of his hand had it espaliered across his skull to cover his baldness.

"Effie!" he said, and stood drinking up the charm of blue hair, blue gown, blue eyes, and white cheeks, for they had faded at his entrance.

"Arthur!" she answered, similarly enthralled with her view.

Daphne stared in patent disbelief at this dwarf, whom she was accustomed to hearing spoken of both at home and at Effie's as a "fine figure of a man." Love was indeed blind in this case.

"You've changed," he said, his black eyes darting all over Effie.

Miss Ingleside felt he was in no case himself to be finding fault with the ravages of time wrought on the once-beautiful Effie but soon realized her error. "You're prettier than ever!" he declared at the end of his inspection. He bounced forward to grab Effie's dimpled arms in his brown hands and shake her in a transport of delight.

"You've changed, too, Arthur," was her aunt's besotted reply, its dulcet tone and attendant smiles removing any hint that the change had not been for the better. "You're wearing your hair differently."

Daphne assumed he had not been wearing it so

sparsely when he was a young man.

"Aye, and you've changed your hair, too," Arthur told her with a critical glance. "It looks nice. Blue always suited you best."

"You didn't use to think so, Arthur," Effie teased him with a coy smile.

"Now don't you get to teasing me about the skirts so soon, naughty puss. I never look at one these days." As he spoke he espied Daphne looking at him, and his sharp black eyes began making an assessment of her charms.

"Well, I always liked blue," Effie said, but the words themselves conveyed nothing. All was in the tone, the smile, the white and brown fingers that were now entwined.

"Who's the young lady?" Arthur demanded, trying to give his full attention to them both at once.

"This is my sister Mary's girl, Miss Ingleside," Effie said.

Arthur felt he had been short-changed to have been deprived of the mother's acquaintance all these years but was ready to make it up with the daughter.

"You're very like your aunt, you know," he congratulated Daphne.

"Thank you, Sir. So I have been told. I expect you two have many things to talk over, and I shall retire now. I am pleased to have met you, Lord Standington."

"We'll certainly be meeting again," he said, smacking his lips in anticipation.

As she left the room, Daphne heard Arthur turn

to Effie and tease her. "Now what's this nonsense I read about you writing a book? All a hum, I suppose. You never *could* write."

Thirteen

DAPHNE crept up to her room noiselessly so as not to disturb the lovers, who she was convinced were staging a reconciliation in the Blue Saloon. She was happy for Effie—it was what she had wanted for the past thirty years, and it gave her aunt a place to go where she would be welcome. It would have been difficult to convince Papa to take her in, particularly if he heard of the mangle they had made of this Season in London. But he would not hear—he would be told only that Effie was to remarry Lord Standington and so Daphne had decided to return home. It gave her an unexceptionable excuse to do so, and she would be spared the holiday at Bath, which held no novel charms for her as it was only ten miles from her own home and a spot familiar to her without having any particularly pleasant associations. Its valetudi-

narian population was of only minimal interest to
a healthy young girl. Effie was a large-hearted
lady to forgive Standington for divorcing her and
leaving it to another man to defend her honour, but
she was not blameless herself, either. Daphne
hoped the marriage would take this time.

She looked at her clock—it was nine-thirty and
she was in no hurry to face a sleepless night. Aunt
Effie might expect her to go belowstairs to
congratulate them a little later, and for this reason
she delayed getting undressed and spent the next
half hour folding up her lingerie preparatory to
packing for her trip home. She worked slowly, her
mind wandering off on strange tangents that left
her standing for five minutes with a nightgown
hanging from her fingers while her eyes looked off
into the distance, seeing things that never were
and, she feared, never would be.

It was after ten o'clock when a servant tapped
on her door and said there was a caller to see her in
the study. She didn't have to enquire who the caller
was. She hadn't had but one for the past several
days. She knew as surely as Effie had known
Arthur was coming that St. Felix was downstairs,
waiting to scold her once again. She went with a
remarkably light heart to hear the chastisement.

Had she thought about it for a moment, she
would have known he would be in full evening
dress, having come from his sister's ball; but she
pictured him, as she always saw him, in day
clothing and was surprised to find him all in black,
looking even more elegant than usual, every inch
the duke, and very severe. She was no sooner
inside the door than he turned his dark, wrathful

eyes on her and stared in silence for half a minute. When he spoke, it was not in the tone of a tirade with which she was familiar and well able to deal, but in low, offended accents. "Why didn't you come?" he asked. "You promised me you would be there." She had to listen closely to hear him.

"You know it was impossible. We read in the paper this morning of your mother's arrival in town."

"All the more reason. I most particularly want her to meet you."

"I don't suppose you particularly want her to meet my aunt."

"She has met your aunt and has no objection to doing so again. And, in any case, that was no excuse for *you* to stay away."

"I couldn't very well go alone."

"You know I would have been happy to come for you. You could have sent me a note—let me know of your change of plans."

"I meant to tell you when you came—that is—I thought you might drop around during the day, as you have been doing."

"It was impossible for me to come. I haven't had a minute to spare the whole day long. I hardly had time to get into my evening costume. It's only ten o'clock. There is still time."

"No, no. I am not ready for the ball, and it's after ten o'clock. My hair not done and nothing to wear."

"You have a gown—you planned to come as late as yesterday," he pointed out angrily.

"Well, I am not wearing my gown and couldn't possibly get ready in time. Go back to your sister's—you shouldn't have left."

"I am not leaving till you agree to come with me," he said, and, walking to the chair, he sat down and crossed his legs and arms, as if to stay the night if necessary.

"Oh, how stubborn you are! Don't think to push me into going there looking a quiz, for I shan't do it." Yet every bone in her body wanted to do just that.

"If you stay here, I stay, and it is a very nice party we are missing. I was looking forward to dancing with you. You promised me you would see me dance to your tune, too."

"I didn't mean at a ball."

"Call Aunt Effie. We'll let her decide."

"No, we can't disturb her. Oh—I didn't tell you! Lord Standington arrived an hour ago, and they are cooing like lovebirds in the Blue Saloon."

"Is he indeed here?" he asked. This news was sufficiently interesting to prod him out of his pucker. "You think he means to take her back?"

"Yes, and it beats me why she should have him, for he is a midget. I always pictured him more—I don't know. Taller, and more handsome. He is a very toadstool of a man."

"But no mushroom. A fine old family, and well to grass, too. Effie needs that. It would be the making of her if he'd marry her again."

"I am convinced he came for no other reason."

"I'm delighted to hear it. But about *my* reason for coming?"

"Your reason has less chance of prospering. None, in fact."

Seeing she was adamant, he changed his tack. "May I bring Mama here, then?"

"When, tonight?"

"Yes, right away."

"You can't bring her *here*."

"Then come with me. Everyone is asking for you."

"And assuming, no doubt, that I was not invited."

"Perhaps at first, but the family has been at considerable pains to let the world know you have been induced to accept, and I cannot believe you will be cut on this occasion."

"No, for I shan't be there to give the world another chance."

"You are too hard on the world. Every dog is allowed his one bite. Give the city another chance, as you gave me."

"Yes, and I still don't see why you first came here determined to despise and insult me. Why should I take so much abuse sitting down?"

"I hadn't observed you to be doing much sitting down in the matter. But about my own behaviour, it was anger that led me to perform so abominably—anger with myself. When you find yourself liking someone you know you should by rights hate, you become angry with yourself and vent your ire on the other. It is not an uncommon thing, I believe."

"I never heard anything so nonsensical in my life," she objected, pretending not quite to grasp the import of his words.

"Have you not? And here I thought you might be

experiencing the same sensation." He regarded her levelly.

"I wonder what Lord Standington can be saying to Auntie," she remarked irrelevantly.

"Whatever it is, he's saying it in a mighty soft voice."

Daphne walked to the door of the study and looked into the hall, just in time to see Standington and Effie emerge from the Blue Saloon, wreathed in smiles and still holding hands like a pair of love-sick youths.

"Daphne, you'll never guess what!" Effie said.

"It won't take me three guesses," Daphne laughed. "Congratulations, to you both."

"She has the gift, too," Arthur said to his bride-to-be. St. Felix looked lost, but no one explained the mystery to him.

"We're to get married right away and go back to Ireland," Effie continued with her good news. "How happy I shall be to get away from here, and really I was not looking forward to Bath in the least."

"Brighton is where you should have gone, goose," Standington told her, but his attention was at least half for Daphne.

"Indeed, it is, for besides Bath being so close to James and Mary—not that I would mind seeing Mary, of course—but James, you know... And there are all those invalids wheeling around in their chairs, taking up the whole sidewalk."

"I am very happy for you," Daphne said, kissing her aunt's cheek and offering her hand to Arthur, who reached up and helped himself to the fine young wench's cheek. "A regular dasher," he was thinking.

"And you're to come with us—no arguments!" Arthur said, more aware by the moment of the beauty of his bride's niece.

"Oh—oh, that sounds lovely," Daphne said, startled at the idea of sharing their honeymoon but not yet on to Arthur's passion for her. He kept up a good show of leering at Effie, too.

St. Felix felt the ground shifting beneath his feet and, like his father before him, was rapidly becoming a foe of Lord Standington. But he shook hands and offered congratulations civilly while his mind raced to adjust itself to the new state of affairs. Effie and Standington soon returned to the Blue Saloon and St. Felix, putting his hand on Daphne's elbow, steered her towards the study.

"You won't like Ireland at this time of the year," he said firmly.

"Spring is the best time of the year, and it can't be worse than London at any season."

"You will find it cold and damp—the houses all draughty and the food deplorable. The people are rude and ill-spoken." He had been to Ireland twice and liked it very much. "You would do better to stay in England. Come to Mama and myself in Kent if you don't wish to return home yet."

"Kent is the last place I could go."

"The countryside is beautiful. Kent is the garden of England you know. My house is large and comfortable. I keep a full stable—plenty of ladies' mounts, for I often receive my sisters; and the food, prepared by my French chef, is excellent.

And the host and hostess would do all in their power to make you feel welcome."

"Thank you, but I have never been to Ireland. I am convinced the travel would be broadening."

"You saw the way Standington was looking at you! Why do you think he wants you there?"

"To help him reach books and things off tall shelves perhaps," she replied, laughing. "And don't you dare to suggest I am in danger of ruin from my aunt's little tiny husband."

"Come now, quit prevaricating with me. You know perfectly well what I am trying to say."

"You are not usually without more direct words, Your Grace. What are you trying to say?"

"Marry me. Is that direct enough?" he asked sharply.

"What a perfectly ridiculous idea!" she said, and didn't even notice his imperative manner of phrasing his offer of marriage.

"So it is, but everyone else finds the ridiculous custom of marriage acceptable. All the go—they are stumbling over each other to get buckled at this time of the year. Effie means to have a fourth go at it."

"I suppose we could always get divorced if it didn't work out," she said with a sly smile.

"Why not? You deprived us of the mud lustre of scandal for our family escutcheon. You could at least give us a divorce and set yourself up in style to pen that epilogue you are preparing notes for."

"You tempt me, Your Grace."

"Good. What other temptations can I include? A honeymoon in Ireland, a flirtation with the toadstool, one slightly used duke who loves you very much, the moon, a voucher to Almack's...

"And the sun, I think, for good measure."

"Several sons, and a daughter, as well. It has been brewing for years that a St. Felix marry one of you upstart baronet's daughters. Let's have it over and done with, or I'll end up trailing across the country to Wiltshire at your skirts."

"Picking up an actress along the way."

"Laying my son open to blackmail. You see what horrors lie before us. No, truly Daphne!" his bantering tone became more serious. "I want very much to marry you. Will you have me?"

"You can't marry me. My reputation is in a shambles. I can't even think straight. Maybe later—"

"Now! I'll do the thinking for both of us, and I think we should suit very well. No, no, give your poor disordered brain a rest," he urged as she opened her mouth to voice some objection. "I further think we should beat Effie and Standington to it. Why should she chalk up four before we have even one to our credit?"

She was laughing openly now in delight at his eagerness, and he took advantage of this rare show of good humour on her part to proceed to action. He drew her into his arms and said, "Termagant!" in a fierce tone before he kissed her with a certain pleasing display of violence.

"Really, St. Felix!" she breathed when she managed to struggle free.

"As good as an acceptance. Already you treat me with a connubial contempt. I am usually given the full benefit of being 'Your Grace'. I'll be 'the old man' before many days are out."

"No, no! I had thought to make it Mr. P. as your name is Percival. So much more refined."

"Certainly it is. I like it enormously, Mrs. P.," he said, and with a soft laugh he enfolded her in his arms to kiss her breath away.

"You had best go back to the ball," she reminded him some few moments later.

"I've been thinking about that."

"That gives me a marvelous idea of your romanticism—worrying about missing a ball while you propose to me!"

"It was an excellent opportunity to miss, but I think that, all things considered, it might be better to wait and see what use we can make of your aunt's marriage. It will be well to have her reestablished to some sort of respectability. And it will be less onerous for both herself and Mama if they meet under this new circumstance, I think."

"There is no husband for Effie to steal this time."

"No, but one for Mama to have a crack at! We'll have the Standingtons bring you to my ball and perhaps announce our engagement there. With Effie on the verge of leaving for Ireland, people won't think it worth while to feud with her."

"They might think it worth while to go on hating me, though."

"No one hates you, except possibly Brummell, and I fancy he's only piqued that you got the best of him in a few verbal battles. *Try* if you can control your tongue, shrew! I must go. Don't do anything atrocious before morning, if you please."

"As *I* am to spend the remainder of the evening alone in my room, I think it is *you* who had better beware of doing anything atrocious."

"You wouldn't be sitting alone in your room if you'd done as I told you. Let this be a lesson to you!" he wagged an admonitory finger under her nose. "I promise I shan't dance with any but the ugliest ladies in the room—all the Patronesses of Almack's and their crones, to butter them up for next year. And, of course, the Ministers' wives, to thank them for letting Larry into the club."

"You don't mean Sir Lawrence has been made a member of the Cabinet!"

"Yes, he was told this afternoon. It is to be in tomorrow's paper. Minister of the Colonies. They figure he can't do any worse than the King, who managed to lose the American colonies for us. Can't you see Bess setting up a salon in the wilds of Canada?"

"Will they have to go there?"

"No, ignoramus! The Cabinet meets in London. I doubt Larry would even know which direction to head his boat if they sent him to the colonies. And now once again I am to head myself in the direction of Charles Street. South from here, isn't it? My head is in a whirl. Oh—shall we be married here or in Wiltshire?"

"We'd best go home. You will have to see Papa."

He pulled a letter from his pocket. "Oh, no, I have *carte blanche* by mail to do with you as I see fit, but it would look better if your family were on hand for the nuptials, and I daresay you would prefer it. Besides, your mama added a post script that I don't quite understand—something about not hurrying, but I think she referred to gowns and not the wedding."

"When did you write to Papa?"

"Just a few days ago—the day I got back from Kent. He must have sat down on the moment and written off his agreement. Very happy to be rid of you. Are you quite sure you had all those beaux in Wiltshire at your feet? I begin to fear they thought you destined for the shelf, to have handed you over by mail."

She looked dismayed at these unflattering statements. "But they were not half so eager to be rid of you as I am to take you in hand," he assured her with a searching look.

A hand flew to her mouth. *"Take me in hand!* Just like Papa—and Standington, and all the very worst husbands. Oh, what have I done?"

"You've cooked your own goose, Mrs. P.," he answered with a quizzing smile. "Too late to wiggle out of it now, but if you behave with some semblance of propriety and eat up all your meat and potatoes, I shan't be so very hard on you."

"How strange," she said, wondering that Effie should have passed up St. Felix's father for that dumply little lecher sitting with her in the Blue Saloon. If one were so foolish as to take on a tyrant and a dictator for a husband, he ought at least to be a tall, handsome tyrant.

"Very strange," he agreed, with no notion what she was talking about but with an idea that his mother and sister would be worried at his absence from the ball. "Are you certain you won't put on your gown and come with me?" he asked one last time.

"No, you had best go."

"I don't want to." He kissed both her hands.

"Well, but I think you had better."

"Now we see who really gives the orders around here!" He touched his forehead with his fingers and left.

Fourteen

ST. Felix did exactly as he had promised and danced with all the stiff old matrons, into whose ears he whispered compliments, interspersed with words of praise for Miss Ingleside, who unfortunately had the migraine this evening, as she had on the occasion of the last meeting of Almack's. It was nearly morning when the party broke up, and though the whole family wanted only to go to bed, St. Felix made them assemble in the Gold Saloon for a parley as to how they must all proceed in the following days. It was, strangely, from Sir Lawrence Thyrwite that an idea was culled.

"Standington here, you say?" he asked. "Liverpool will be happy to hear it. One more vote for the Conservatives. He always votes with the Prince of Wales, you know. Prinney was speaking of creating a few more Tory peers to get the Reform

Bill modified and to get his latest Civil List passed."

"Be sure to tell them both Standington is in town," St. Felix said.

"Yes, the Prince will want to invite him to his do at Carlton House. Having a bit of a party tomorrow night. Not precisely in my honour, but I believe a toast is to be drunk to my promotion." Lawrence and Bess both glowed with triumph and glory, and, indeed, the family was very well pleased with this new honour bestowed on one of their members.

"Excellent. *I* shall take you, Mama," St. Felix went on. "Don't pout, I know you don't like to go there, but I will only ask it of you this once. Bess and Larry, you take Uncle Algernon with you. Mama and I will round up the other relatives—the Dowager Marchioness of Monmouth must be routed out, and Lord Skeffington. When the Standington party arrives, we will make much to do about them. A great deal depends on those first few moments."

"Will Miss Ingleside be there?" his mother asked, eager for a look at the girl.

"She'll go with Standington's party. I'll arrange it."

"Don't see why you couldn't marry some respectable girl if you've decided to swap rings," Larry complained. "Lady Barbara would have had you."

"But I am engaged to Miss Ingleside," St. Felix pointed out.

"I know that! Ain't a complete fool. A minister of the Government, after all. Didn't have to go getting engaged to her. That Pealing woman—not the thing." Upon becoming a minister, Larry had raised his standards of respectability, and Effie's heart of gold had ceased to excite his admiration.

"There's nothing wrong with Countess Standington!" Uncle Algernon took up the cudgels in her defence. "And you didn't think so yourself twenty years ago."

"Twenty-five! I was only a boy. I didn't know any better."

"Well *she* did! She knew enough not to give you a look-in, and that's what's bothering you now."

"There is no need to rake up all that ancient history!" Bess intervened.

"I want it all raked up and buried once and for all," St. Felix said. "I don't mean to bring Daphne into a family where she is looked down on and whispered about behind her back. We all know about the aunt—she has caused a good deal of bother in this family one way or another, but not nearly so much as she could have caused—and it has nothing to do with Miss Ingleside."

"She has caused enough bother on her own," Bess said, cross at her husband's rough treatment from Uncle Algernon.

"She wouldn't have caused any bother if the men of this house hadn't all made fools of themselves over Mrs. Pealing," St. Felix adjured.

"She came here to blackmail us!" Bess reminded him.

"Countess Standington never did anything of the sort," Algernon shouted, jumping to his feet and promptly sitting down again as a stab of gout racked his knee. "And neither did her niece!" he insisted, without knowing a thing about it.

A fine family brawl ensued for the better part of an hour, with Algernon calling Sir Lawrence a drooling idiot, Sir Lawrence reciprocating the compliment by pointing out that Algernon had never been made a minister or anything else of any importance, Bess dissolving into tears, and the Dowager saying she was glad her husband wasn't alive to see them all acting such a Cheltenham tragedy over nothing. The whole mess was thoroughly hashed over, raked up, and buried. When they were finally allowed to leave, they were all back in spirits, with Lawrence promising to send Uncle Algernon a very interesting report on the fur trade in Canada to look over (and hopefully explain to him, for it seemed very complicated). They were each fully aware of the roles they were to play in the coming days.

The Dowager Duchess of St. Felix and her son drove in the Park with Miss Ingleside the following afternoon and left off an announcement of the engagement at three newspaper offices, having decided to let the shock waves subside before their ball. In the evening a large party was assembled at Carlton House, where the Prince Regent was polite to Lord Standington, taking him aside to explain which party they were supporting this year and that Lord Standington's attendance at a few sessions of the House was highly desirable to defeat those rabble-rousing Whigs. Castlereagh flattered the Irish lord into believing he knew what was going on in the sphere of politics and said he was delighted to finally make the acquaintance of Lady Standington, endowing Effie with her old, and soon to be new, title for the occasion.

Prinney coyly took Effie's hand and said, "I see now why you turned me off, sly puss. But you might have told me what was in the wind. I was very much hurt at your treatment of me."

"Oh, Your Highness—it is no such a thing," she began. Happily, she was then struck with a thought rather than a feeling and realized that his vanity might be wonderfully salved by this face-saving explanation. "I could not tell you before Standington arrived. I promised him I would not. How rattled I was when you came to my apartment. I hardly knew what to say—such an honour!"

"No need to say a word. I understand, my dear Countess." The Prince, too, gave her the dignity of her old title, but his roving eye was soon intercepting a smile from the charming Lady Conyngham and he waddled off in her direction.

Standington, too, received a few encouraging glances from the shorter ladies present and felt he could put up with London for a week or so. It was clear to the onlookers at the party that Mrs. Pealing was to be counted amongst their friends, and before she left she had three invitations to tea and four callers asking exactly where on Grosvenor Square her apartment was to be found.

Miss Ingleside was found to be charming, and as no one was rude to her, she got through the night without saying a sharp word to anyone. She was disappointed to see Mr. Brummell was not there but was told by her groom that Carlton House was the last spot in London one would expect to see him.

The Beau was no longer welcome at the Regent's residence, which made it very necessary for him to read all reports of happenings there. He read with mixed emotions that Miss Ingleside and Mrs. Pealing had been amongst the guests and sat down to compose a few remarks worthy of the young Incognita when next they came to cuffs. That she was to marry St. Felix was also read and digested, and when finally he confronted her at Lord St. Felix's ball, to which he had been invited at the express wish of the young lady, he was ready for her.

"I am delighted to see you are back amongst us. London was desolate without you."

"I haven't been away. In fact, I was at a party at Carlton House this week."

He knew it well and had his reply ready. "That is as good—or as bad—as being out of the city. *I* no longer go there, you see."

"You could hardly do so without an invitation."

"I have let His Highness know the futility of sending invitations to me. You don't want to become too close to him—bad *ton*. But you have made a much better alliance, I hear, with the Duke of St. Felix."

"A grand enough match that I took the risk of inviting *you* to our ball, Mr. Brummell."

"And *I* took the risk of accepting, for the pleasure of your conversation. One must live a little precariously." His insolence, delivered in drawling accents with a half-smile on his face, did not goad her into anger any longer. He was really rather pitiful.

"Don't live too precariously, Mr. Brummell. I

would miss you if I should wake up one morning and find the King of Absurdity had been dethroned."

"You are too kind, but I fear the King is more likely to be decapitated than dethroned. St. Felix is looking daggers at me. The fellow is a fiend of jealousy, you know. I must drop you a word of warning."

"When you undertake to counsel me on how to deal with my husband, you are really overstepping the bounds, Mr. Brummell."

"It is commonly said my impertinence knows no bounds, Ma'am. But my discretion does, and I shall take my leave before he comes. Good evening. I look forward to meeting you again, very soon."

He scraped a leg and left, with a warm smile on his petulant lips, to have a word with Lady Melbourne and plan new mischief.

"Setting up a flirtation with the Beau?" St. Felix asked. "I wondered at your eagerness to have him here."

"I owe him a few debts but find them devilish hard to pay off. What a tongue the man has."

"That must recommend him to you, no doubt, but I have someone else who wishes for your acquaintance. My Uncle, the Archbishop of Canterbury," he explained, and led her to make the acquaintance.

The honour granted, Daphne asked, "Did you actually present Aunt Effie to the Archbishop?"

"It was not in the least necessary. He used to be one of her court twenty-odd years ago, when he was only an archdeacon. I notice Standington is keeping a sharp eye on him. Quite an infamous lady, that aunt of yours. It is as well she is to be taken to Ireland."

"There isn't room in London for two of us black ewes."

"I mean to do a much better job of keeping you in line than old Standington did with your aunt," he informed her sternly.

"I am used to dealing with you tyrants. Papa was just such another, and you will recall my trick to get him to let me come to London."

"You are welcome to come to London whenever you please, so long as I come with you, or so long as you behave yourself."

"How dull—to come with my husband and to behave myself. I might as well stay locked up with the flowers in Kent."

"I didn't say you must do both—you may misbehave yourself as much as you like, so long as you do it with me. Shall we slip out the door for a little misbehaviour now? There is a nice private morning parlour just around the corner in the hall that might have been made for the purpose."

"It likely was, if your ancestors were anything like yourself."

"We know what a model of propriety Papa was. The room I am speaking of is right here." He took her elbow and walked to an elegant little parlour hung in blue velvet draperies with a blue carpet.

"This looks as if Effie might have had a hand in decorating it," she said, and felt very much at home in the room. "Or *some* lady with a fondness for blue, in any case," she added with a pert smile.

"Who knows? Father may have had it done to please your aunt. It is clear, I think, that the room has not been redecorated recently, and not, I assure you, by any friend of mine. Papa tried to give Effie a blue ring once, you know."

"It is reassuring to know such a wide streak of fidelity runs in the family I am about to join."

"Faithful to the very marrow of the bones. Papa's mistake was in marrying before he met Effie, I suppose. *I* have been more fortunate. What a man should do is marry the woman he would want to make his mistress. It gets rid of a lot of problems."

"That rather depends on his taste in mistresses. I foresee a few difficulties if certain gentlemen were to marry their present flirts."

"We are talking about *you*. I foresee no difficulties."

"Is that supposed to be a compliment?"

"If you choose to take it as one. It is a roundabout way of saying I won't make my father's mistakes. You are the only woman I want, or have ever wanted."

"Amy will be sorry, and surprised, I wager, to hear it," she said with a lift of her brows.

"She was not surprised—*was* not, you notice. I have cleared up all the loose ends."

"How thorough of you!" she congratulated him with a breath of relief.

"I believe in doing things thoroughly," he replied, and, drawing her into his arms, he kissed her very thoroughly, indeed.